The Heart Broker

A dramatic and distinctly terrifying story!

by Colin Vard

Cover Illustration by Tony Kew

Celtpress

Celtpress Ltd.
Kindlestown Hill
Delgany
Co. Wicklow
Republic of Ireland
Tel/Fax: (01) 287 3026

ISBN 1-897973-04-7

*All the characters in this book are fictitious.
Any resemblance to actual persons, living or dead,
is purely coincidental.*

Printed by Vision Print
Unit 3, Blackrock Business Centre
Brookfield Terrace
Blackrock, Co. Dublin

CHAPTER 1

"I want my wife!... Catherine, why don't you answer me? ... Can you not hear me? ... Catherine ... Oh, Catherine. Where are you now when I need you?"

The anguished cries came from a despairing old man. His face was lined like the crusted bark of an oak tree. His plea echoed around the ward. Those who had visited the hospital since Seán had been admitted had grown accustomed to his shrill outbursts.

"I called her this morning, Mr. McAvoy. She had some shopping to do. She will call in after lunch."

"You wouldn't lie to me, nurse, would you?" the emaciated old man queried hopefully as the smiling Nurse Yeats drew adrenaline into a syringe and placed the needle in a narrow vein in his arm.

"Of course not. I scarcely have time to tell the truth."

The old man relaxed and closed his eyes.

Dr. Joan Curry, an attractive dark-haired heart specialist, was covering for a colleague. The Director of the National Cardiac Surgery Unit was at a conference in Mexico. She watched anxiously from across the ward. She came and stood at the end of Seán's bed. He had been found Sunday morning wandering alone and confused around Parnell Square. He was breathing easier now, but his pulse was slowing. Dr. Curry picked up his chart.

To the staff and doctors of the Mater Hospital, Dr. Curry was as astringent as her name suggested. No other authority in the hospital was more respected and feared. She had come through the system without favours. She was ageless.

"He isn't!" Nurse Yeats declared.

"Isn't what?" demanded Dr. Curry impatiently.

"Married of course!"

Dextrose and saline dripped slowly into the old man's veins, feeding his tissues. The bed was warm. His head and shoulders had been elevated to make his breathing easier. For a moment his eyes opened searching the room.

"Catherine! Catherine!"

"It's all right, Mr. McAvoy. You sleep now. You will feel better when you wake."

Dr. Curry replaced the chart and retreated to the door. Nurse Yeats withdrew a withered calf from beneath the bedclothes. She began to massage Seán's legs, trying to help the blood circulate through his limp veins.

As Dr. Curry reached the door there was a raucous scream from behind. Nurse Yeats pulled back the curtain and beckoned to Dr. Curry. Seán sat upright gasping for air. Dr. Curry ran to his bedside, placed her stethoscope against the old man's chest and tapped her fingers on his chest wall.

"Help me doctor!" croaked old Seán, "I can't b ... b ... breathe."

Dr. Curry placed the oxygen mask over Seán's mouth. His cries were muffled. His face was turning blue and his body was cold to the touch. The only sound now was the hissing of the oxygen. Dr. Curry looked at Nurse Yeats and forced a reassuring smile.

"All is not lost, nurse!"

ఇ ఇ ఇ

Dr. Curry's mind wandered beyond the Mater hospital to a small field hospital high in the Andes close to Cuzco in Peru. Dr. Declan McNamee fought to save the life of a young boy. Behind him stood a man aiming a semi-automatic rifle at Declan's head.

Ten months ago, Declan and Joan had travelled to the small mission carved out of a damp, misty rain forest to work for a charitable organisation operated by a Jesuit priest. Declan was an uncanny doctor with few equals. He knew what to look for and, more importantly, he took the time to find it. Joan recalled the day an old woman was taken into the small makeshift hospital. Declan suspected that she had a dangerously dilated blood-vessel sac which, if it could be located, might be removed surgically. If not, it would almost certainly haemorrhage with fatal consequences. For an hour Declan sat observing the sick woman's chest and abdomen as she slept. Finally, he suggested that they turn the bed around. Declan moved to the window, raised the bamboo blind, then sat again watching his patient from a different angle in a new light. Within minutes, he was on his feet pointing to a spot on the woman's chest wall. There, faintly, but at the same time unmistakably shadowed by the slanting afternoon sunshine, was the telltale pulsation.

In the grime and misery of this mountain top hospital, Declan and Joan performed major surgery, often without anaesthesia. Once, just after the hospital had been attacked and ransacked by bandits, they had to amputate a small girl's leg with an old razor blade and manicure scissors. Medicines were always scarce, indeed usually non-existent. Declan, through necessity, recalled and utilised primitive medical remedies. For fevers, he roasted animal bones and then ground them into a fine powder. For diarrhoea, he boiled oak bark. Many of the locals suffered from hernias. The remedial operation was difficult and painful to carry out without anaesthesia. Declan recalled, as a young student, reading a paper about medicine in the middle ages and, as suggested in the article, strung up the patient feet first to a branch of a tree. With gravity on his side, he easily manipulated the organs back through the hernial opening.

One night during a torrential rain storm, the door of the infirmary burst open. Standing on the clay floor was an irate and nervous group of men carrying a young boy who had been severely injured by a falling tree. His thigh and skull had been crushed. Declan looked at the pitiful child, limp in his father's arms, then at Joan. It was apparent that two lives now depended on the success of this operation. They had chosen to live on the top of the world in one of the remotest regions of Peru. There was no governing authority and the laws were of nature, not of a modern civilisation. Declan was considered by many of the natives to be an enemy, not a saviour. It was the white man who had cleared the forests and upset the ecological system and Declan was now ultimately held responsible for this seriously injured child.

Declan indicated that the child should be placed on the simple operating table. Without the benefit of x-ray equipment, he set about diagnosing the full extent of the child's injuries. After careful deliberation, he instructed Joan to shave the child's damaged and badly swollen head while he administered an anaesthetic. The child's father stood impassively as Declan opened the shattered leg with a scalpel. With a foot-powered dental drill, he bored holes in the shattered bone before expertly wiring the fragments together with bicycle spokes.

Joan stood back after she had shaved the boys scalp. Without further consideration, Declan poured alcohol on the crown of the boy's head and, with a swift, circular movement, peeled back the boy's scalp with his scalpel. It was obvious as he removed the bone fragments and a piece of damaged brain that if the child survived the trauma he would almost certainly be severely mentally and physically handicapped. Despite all Declan's efforts, the young boy died. Joan cradled his seizure-racked body. The child's father immediately gathered up his dead son. His followers tied and bound Declan, then dragged him out into the storm. Joan was roughly bound with surgical tape and tied with rope to the blood-splattered operating table.

The following morning, when Joan had finally managed to release herself, she made her way down the mountainside. At the bottom of the ravine she found Declan's body.

* * *

Dr. Curry adjusted the flow of oxygen and walked to the foot of Seán's bed.

"Nurse take one leg! I will take the other!" Both nurse and doctor began a slow, rhythmic upward massage. When they had finished, Dr. Curry studied Seán's vital signs.

"Nurse sponge him with warm alcohol. I am going to try digitalis."

Dr. Curry removed the oxygen mask. The colour in the old man's face had improved. His breathing was deeper. She injected digitalis, which took immediate effect. The stimulated heart beat faster. Seán's eyes roved the room in desperation. His bony hands grasped the bed sheets tightly. His face was turning blue again. He began to gurgle. His pulse was weakening. The thermometer read over 104°. In desperation and confusion, Nurse Yeats threw back the bed covers and began to sponge his wasted body. He stopped breathing … Nurse Yeats turned to Dr. Curry. Seán's body shuddered and went still … There was a long pause. He began to breathe again. Each forced breath seemed to be his last. Dr. Curry filled the syringe with strychnine. With her fingers trembling, she pressed the plunger. Ashen-faced, both nurse and doctor waited for the drug to take effect.

The pulse beneath Dr. Curry's fingers beat strongly. Relieved, Dr. Curry sat at the end of Seán's bed.

Outside it was dark. Night had fallen. Seán's breathing was shallow, his heart sound was faint, listless. His death was inevitable. Nurse Yeats went about her duties.

A bleeper sounded from the bank of monitoring equipment. Seán had stopped breathing again. Dr. Curry stood patiently waiting for his breathing to resume. Seán stared sightlessly at the hospital ceiling. Dr. Curry injected more strychnine. Silence ... There was a rustling sound like dry leaves being scattered by a breeze. Seán's emaciated body shivered and rattled. Soon afterwards, the rattle came again. This time it was louder and more shocking. Then silence. For Seán, it was eternal.

Nurse Yeats pulled the sheet over Seán's head. His bony wrist, which had been gripping the sheet, fell lifeless onto the mattress. This was not the first time Dr. Curry had witnessed death but, despite her years of experience, she was never passive or complacent. She was a highly skilled specialist. Her job was to prolong life.

ぁ ぁ ぁ

Before she left the hospital, Joan checked on a seriously ill young patient of the director's. James was a handsome sandy-haired boy of eighteen. He stared at Joan through dazed and fearful eyes. His young attractive mother sat alone, nervously twisting a tattered handkerchief. Aside from drowsiness due to medication, the boy seemed healthy, if withdrawn. While Joan examined him he remained tense and silent, offering no resistance.

"I know that I am sick doctor ... Will I ever get better? Am I ... Am I going to die? I want to be strong. I want my father to be proud of me."

James drifted to sleep. His mother turned away, embarrassed. Dr. Curry noted that it was a strange, guileless remark from a frightened child. It seemed to her that James was fearful for his father's sake and not his own. In his mind, his sickness was a failure.

Dr. Curry's intuition suggested child abuse. Her examination all but confirmed it. James, she feared, would die if he did not receive a donor heart soon.

                       ن. ن. ن.

At home, in her luxury fourth floor penthouse apartment on Killiney Hill, Joan, once a woman of great inner strength, was now questioning her resolve. She looked out over the panoramic vista of lights that shrouded Dublin City at night-time. Since she had returned alone from Peru, she had spent many nights like this. Dublin, once a vibrant place of excitement, adventure and hope, now imprisoned and strangled her. Joan selected a Nick Cave compact disc, *Tender Prey*. She sat in the gloom and reflected while the tortured sounds emanating from the speakers washed over her.

> *And the mercy seat is waiting*
> *And I think my head is burning*
> *And in a way I'm yearning*
> *To be done with all the measuring of truth.*
> *An eye for an eye, a tooth for a tooth.*
> *And I'm not afraid to die.*

Joan was a tall, angular woman with shoulder length nut brown hair worn in a plait. She was an only child. Her father and his younger brother were lost at sea in a fishing tragedy off Dunmore East. Their bodies were never

7

recovered. That was twenty-five years ago. Joan was only five at the time. The community in Dunmore, where Joan lived, never spoke of the tragedy. Two years later, her mother died in a traffic accident. Joan went to live with her aunt and cousin, Eileen, in Dungarvan.

Since Declan was murdered in Peru, Joan had chosen to live alone. Many of her colleagues unfairly accused her of wallowing in self pity.

Her nightmare had begun with a distressing phone call. She had just come off duty and crawled into bed when the phone rang.

"This is the garda station here in Portlaoise. My name is Sergeant John Dunne. I wish to speak to a Miss Joan Curry."

"This is Joan Curry," Joan replied, glancing at her alarm clock. It was five past three in the morning.

"I am sorry to disturb you, miss. A woman believed to be a relation of yours, Miss Eileen Curry, has been involved in a fatal car accident on the town by-pass. You are registered as her next of kin. Could I ask you to call to the station first thing tomorrow morning? We need you to identify the remains."

"Yes, of course," Joan answered in disbelief.

"Good night, miss."

A month later at a solicitor's office in Fitzwilliam Square, Eileen's will was disclosed. Joan learned, to her surprise, that Eileen, a secretary with a Dublin-based oil exploration company, had left Joan shares in that company. Joan knew little about exploration companies and less about shares but Eileen's solicitor valued the shares at what he described as "Quite a considerable sum". Joan, so overcome with grief, did not hear a word.

Three weeks later, Joan qualified as a doctor and celebrated by becoming engaged to Declan McNamee, a tall, dark, well-muscled, handsome doctor from Donegal. Three weeks later, as a result of a chance meeting with a missionary priest in Grafton Street, Declan and Joan deferred their wedding plans and, instead, travelled to Peru with the young Jesuit priest. They were to spend a year working in a small field hospital high in the Andes.

After Declan's death, Joan requested a transfer home. On the day her replacement arrived, she made the long, arduous, five hundred mile expedition back to Lima through dense forests, over dusty dirt tracks and along bandit-infested highways.

ϡ ϡ ϡ

Back in Dublin, and alone in her apartment, Joan opened a large buff-coloured envelope that had arrived while she had been in Peru. Enclosed were share certificates for Skelling Exploration and an accompanying letter from her late cousin's solicitor.

Miss Curry, might I offer the following advice. Exploration shares are not for widows and orphans I strongly advise that you should sell these shares at the first opportunity. If you do not have a stockbroker, might I suggest R.M. & P. Stockbrokers. They are a young, go-ahead company hungry for business and I believe that their senior partner, Raymond Mackin, is by all accounts an extremely competent and personable young man.

Joan knew little about the stock market other than that, if you purchased a share through a stockbroker, you were buying part-ownership of a limited public company. These shares could then be bought and sold on the open market at a profit or loss. The share values were printed daily in the national press.

On the car radio on the way home from the solicitor's office, Joan listened to the reporter stating that A.I.B. was up two, Bank of Ireland down one. She never fully understood what the man from the National Irish Bank meant. The following morning at nine a.m., as the shutters were raised and doors of the book shop opened, Joan Curry entered Eason's in Dun Laoghaire and confidently purchased a book entitled:

Share Millions: How to Make Money on the Stock Market.

"Playing the stock market," the author claimed, "is easy. I make well over seventy-five thousand pounds a year. Believe me, it's far better than working!"

Joan devoured the book, making relevant notes. All she needed was a stockbroker to guide her. On Sunday morning, in the Business Post, she found her stockbroker and to her delight it was the company her solicitor had recommended. R.M. & P. had taken a full page. It looked very impressive. There were photographs of smiling and smartly dressed directors of R.M. & P. in wood panelled boardrooms shaking hands with eminent politicians and chairmen of international companies. It was an advertisement feature, even though the paper certainly did not make this fact clear. The headline declared:

Net profits of five thousand pounds on investments of ten thousand pounds!

Joan was comforted that R.M. & P. appeared to be endorsed by her bank, the National Irish Bank. They were also members of the Irish and International Stock Exchange. Joan was convinced that this was a reputable and well-connected company.

Joan rang R.M. & P. from her office in the hospital first thing on Monday morning. She spoke to a female employee, who appeared competent and helpful.

"Could you hold, please. I think with a portfolio as large as yours I should put you on to one of our senior partners."

The phone went silent for a few moments. Just as Joan was about to hang up and re-dial, an impatient monotone male voice came on the line.

"Good morning. My name is Raymond Mackin. I am the managing director of this company. Our receptionist tells me that you have a few grand to invest. Well, you have come to the right place. Drop in and see me tomorrow and bring details of your portfolio. Let's see ... let me check my diary ... Make it about four thirty."

The phone went dead. Mackin, she thought, appeared inexcusably arrogant! He must be busy, Joan reasoned as she checked the glossary in Share Millions. to see what portfolio meant: "A collection of investments viewed as one entity."

At lunch time, Joan opened the Independent to the business page. There was Skellig listed with all the other exploration shares. It had traded yesterday at forty-one pence. Joan took out her calculator. She sat back, staring in disbelief at the calculator. She never imagined that the shares were worth over one hundred thousand pounds.

That night, Joan passed an exclusive development of apartments on Killiney Hill. She stopped and looked at the wonderful view stretching all the way from Dalkey to Howth. There was an auctioneer's board outside. Joan turned into Killiney Castle Hotel and wrote down the auctioneer's name and phone number: Banks and Co., Greystones 287 4736. She would ring them tomorrow.

"Good morning, Banks and Co.. How may I help you?"

Mr. Bernon was in his mid-thirties and was a dapper, well-spoken, handsome man. He was most enthusiastic about the penthouse apartment on Killiney Hill and arranged to meet Joan at lunch time. Later that afternoon, in the waiting room of R.M. & P., Joan decided to put a deposit on the apartment.

Raymond Mackin appeared an hour late. Without an apology, he ushered Joan into the boardroom. Joan regarded him with disdain, but decided that she was employing his expertise, not his personality. An hour later, she left the offices assured that Raymond Mackin would dispose of her Skellig shares at an agreed price. The arrogant stockbroker added that it may, however, take a couple of weeks to secure the best possible price.

The following morning, Joan rang and made an offer on the apartment. She knew it was an extravagance, but the money from the shares would ease the burden. Mr. Bernon called back later to confirm that the vendor had accepted her offer. Joan made the necessary arrangements with her bank and her solicitor.

ðŁ ðŁ ðŁ

One morning six weeks later, as Joan sat eating breakfast in the kitchen of her penthouse apartment, the postman arrived. There was a letter from R.M. & P. Enclosed was a contract note confirming that her Skellig shares had been sold. Delighted, Joan signed the contract, posted the acceptance in Dalkey and headed into the hospital.

"Scalpel!"

The nurse placed a scalpel in Dr. Curry's palm. The instrument descended, cutting confidently into the patient's abdomen. Dr. Curry's gloved hand groped before lifting and exposing the gallbladder. She slit the sac and three sharp, green-brown stones appeared.

The phone outside the operating room rang. Dr. Curry turned towards the phone, frowned, then nodded to one of the nurses. The nurse stripped off her surgical gloves and answered the phone. Dr. Curry dropped the stones in a basin.

"I cannot disturb Dr. Curry. She is performing an operation at the moment," the nurse declared indignantly before holding the phone away from her ear. Whoever was on the other end had raised their voice.

"I cannot help that!" the nurse repeated. I'm sorry, sir, but she is in the middle of an operation. There is no need to take that tone with me. ... Dr. Curry, there is a Mr. Mackin on the phone. He says that he must speak to you. It is very important!"

"What is it, nurse?" Dr. Curry demanded angrily.

"It is a call for you, Dr. Curry. The man ...!"

"Hang up the phone, nurse!" Dr. Curry demanded.

The nurse gratefully hung up the phone. Before she had put on a fresh pair of gloves, the phone rang again. Dr. Curry pointed to the open cavity.

"I think it will have to come out!" she remarked to a junior surgeon. "I hate to do it. It is a pretty thin wall and he has had trouble. There, look!"

The phone continued to ring. Dr. Curry reluctantly instructed the nurse to answer the phone.

"It is Mr. Mackin again, Dr. Curry!"

Dr. Curry straightened, abruptly turned from the operating table and walked towards the telephone, stripping off her gloves.

"Is that Dr. Joan Curry?" the man's voice queried at the other end of the phone.

"You have interrupted a very important operation," Dr. Curry replied angrily.

"This is Raymond Mackin of R.M. & P. This will only take a second and I presume that you are interested in making money."

Mackin was talking down to Dr. Curry.

"There is an anomaly," he continued, "on the market in London this morning. There is an exploration share called Bedouin. The company is being taken over by Fastnet, another exploration company here in Dublin. The Bedouin share is available at twenty pence. Fastnet have offered Bedouin one Fastnet share for every three Bedouin. Therefore, if you buy three Bedouin shares at a cost of sixty pence, Fastnet will give you one of their shares which is valued at seventy-five pence. Your profit will be fifteen pence per share."

"Dr. Curry, I think you should have a look at this," the anxious junior doctor called to Dr. Curry from the operating table.

"You could clear fifteen thousand pounds in a week," Mackin continued.

Dr. Curry had a festering dislike for Mackin. In medicine nothing, unless it was life-threatening, was entered into without due consideration. As the solicitor advised, shares are not for widows and orphans. Joan, effectively a widow and an orphan, replied.

"Mr. Mackin, I do not wish to purchase these shares. I find your timing and manner inexcusable and I must insist that you refrain from contacting me again during surgery. I am really not interested and I would be obliged if you could forward the monies outstanding from the sale of my Skellig shares to me immediately."

☙ ☙ ☙

On Friday night when Joan arrived home, there was a letter from R.M. & P.. She opened it excitedly. To her dismay, there was no cheque, just a contract note for the purchase of four hundred and fifty thousand Bedouin shares at twenty-one pence and a bill for in excess of one hundred thousand pounds. Joan was bemused and confused. Surely he cannot buy the shares without my permission? Joan turned to the business page in the Irish Independent. The headline read:

Fastnet take-over bid for Bedouin falls through

☙ ☙ ☙

"I'm afraid, Dr. Curry, you are in a very difficult situation."

Joan's solicitor removed his glasses and, in a well-creased navy pinstripe suit, walked to his window overlooking Merrion Square. He carefully folded thin strands of hair over his bald spot. He walked back to the fine hunting table where Joan sat. He placed the R.M. & P. statement of account on the table.

"It is quite simple, doctor. The one hundred thousand pounds that your account was credited with when R.M. & P. sold the Skellig shares your late cousin left you have, quite simply, been debited for a similar amount with the worthless Bedouin shares Mackin purchased on your behalf. Indeed, according to the statement, you actually owe R.M. & P. four thousand pounds for fees and commissions.

"But I did not instruct Mackin to purchase these shares!" Joan banged her fist on the table in anger. "I'm sorry," Joan apologised for her outburst. "What can I do? This man has ruined me! On the strength of the money due

15

to me from the sale of the Skellig shares, I bought the apartment. It appears now that I can't afford it. What on earth can I do?"

"It is, unfortunately, your word against his and possession, as you know, is nine tenths of the law. In good faith, you handed this man your share certificate. What transpired in the interim is, you say, that he purchased these Bedouin shares without your consent. He will claim that you agreed to buy these speculative shares and, now that they have failed to perform, you wish to avoid paying for them. The stock exchange is a volatile marketplace and you were willing to accept the profits from Skellig, but not the loss from Bedouin. I suggest that you go and speak to Mackin and try to reason with him. But be warned. He may be an astute businessman, but he is not known for his compassion. I must also tell you that you are not the first person in the city to have suffered from his dubious dealings. A friend and colleague of mine has defended him on many occasions. Only last week, Mackin settled a claim on the steps of the Four Courts with a disgruntled employee who was sacked because he refused to fraudulently alter client contracts. It appears that Mackin, when instructed, would buy shares on the Dublin market and subsequently alter the contract so that it indicated that the shares had been purchased on the London market in sterling, which, of course, would cost his client more."

Joan's solicitor continued.

"I have had no direct dealings with him, but I remember some time ago having a few late night drinks with a client in Jury's. His brother, who works with him in R.M. & P., arrived and proceeded to buy drinks for everybody at the bar. He boasted that he worked a deal that day which netted him over ten thousand pounds. He had bought and sold a U.K. public placing of water authority shares. I was particularly annoyed at the time, as I myself had contacted R.M. & P. the previous week enquiring about the shares, but was informed that their allocation was limited to three hundred shares per client. At that moment I knew why."

"Why doesn't somebody stand up to him?" Joan enquired reasonably.

"It is strongly rumoured that he is closely linked to a certain arms dealer operating in Bolivia who has considerable influence with national and International subversives. Basically, Dr. Curry, nobody is willing to take the chance. Raymond Mackin is dangerous, ruthless and best avoided."

&ะ &ะ &ะ

"Can I speak to Raymond Mackin please?" Joan's hand shook in anger and fear as she held the phone waiting for Mackin to answer her call.

"Raymond Mackin," the voice bellowed down the phone.

"This is Dr. Joan Curry. I would like to meet with you to discuss my account."

"Yes, you owe me four grand for those shares you bought!" Mackin replied matter-of-factly.

"When are you free to see me?" Joan enquired.

"I don't know why you want to come and see me, but it is your time you are wasting. Two p.m. tomorrow and bring your cheque book." Mackin hung up.

As arranged, at two p.m. the following day, Joan sat nervously in the waiting room of R.M. & P. She read a copy of The Financial Times. The receptionist came in.

"I'm sorry. Mr. Mackin went to a luncheon meeting. He was due back at two."

At three the receptionist returned.

"I called Mr. Mackin. He will be back in fifteen minutes." The receptionist was apologetic, but made no further excuses on Mackin's behalf. It was obvious from this and subsequent meetings that his staff had little respect for him. Joan, however, was not going to be intimidated by this treatment.

At three forty-five — one and three quarter-hours late — Raymond Mackin strode confidently and brazenly into the waiting room without offering an apology. He sat defiantly at the small, circular mahogany table.

"You did not have to wait for me. You could have left the cheque for the money you owe me at reception."

Joan stood and pushed back her chair and pointed her finger at Mackin.

"I am here to demand," Joan replied, infuriated, "that you pay me the money that you received for the sale of my shares. I am certainly not here to pay you the ..."

"How dare you!" Mackin jumped from his chair and lunged at Joan, his mad eyes fired violently. "If you don't pay me by the end of the week, I will issue proceedings against you. Your name will appear in the trade gazettes and national newspapers ... I will also register a judgement mortgage on your three-bedroom penthouse apartment in Killiney. I bet your friends and patients will enjoy reading about you in the papers."

"You leave me no alternative, Mr. Mackin. I am now forced to report you to the stock exchange."

Mackin laughed like a man riddled with insanity.

"You stupid woman. The stock exchange and their regulatory body are powerless. They do just as I tell them. You are taking on more than you can cope with, dear. The best thing you can do is go away and play doctors and nurses, or maybe you would like me to buy some more shares for you?"

Dr. Curry stormed out of R.M.& P. and drove to the hospital. James, the young man she examined the previous day, was deteriorating. His mother appeared alone and desperate. Joan called her into her office. It had a more calming, relaxing ambience. The woman was so emotional that Joan decided to tell her the truth. This would punish her less than her own fantasies. Later, Joan left the hospital despondent. The boy had possibly only days, not weeks, to live.

Dr. Curry sat into her Mazda 323 coupe. As she fastened the seat belt, she watched the rain form in tiny droplets on the shiny black paintwork. She had always felt secure and confident in the car, that is until today. Now it had become another financial burden, just like the apartment. A cold fear passed over her. How did Mackin know that she had purchased a three-bedroom apartment in Killiney?

On the Cabinteely by-pass, Joan was overtaken by an ambulance driving at high speed. There was an accident outside Cabinteely church. A large crowd had gathered. Joan followed the ambulance. The gardai from the local station had just rescued two young joyriders from an angry crowd and dragged them roughly into the station house next to the crashed BMW coupe.

On the roadway, two ambulance men looked in shock at the crumpled and broken body of a man lying motionless in a pool of blood. A priest was giving him the last rites.

CHAPTER 2

"Any calls while I was out?"

Mackin stood close to the young receptionist. Too close. He enjoyed her obvious embarrassment. He was forty-one years old, slim, sallow-skinned and five foot ten. At work he wore a boring navy suit with a matching red silk handkerchief and tie. At leisure he inevitably wore a dark brown pair of slacks and a striped shirt. He was a singularly unattractive man with gaps in his irregular teeth. His mad, sunken eyes and high cheek bones, however, gave him an interesting appearance.

"Your wife called from the hospital. She asked that you contact her. She said it's urgent. Dermot Glanville, the stock exchange regulations manager, also called." The girl picked up her memo pad and read from it, "He wants you to call him the minute you come in. It's very important, he said."

Mackin picked up the pad, tore off the top sheet and dropped it back on the desk.

"Fax Glanville and tell him that you cannot contact me. As far as you know, I have gone away sailing for the week-end. Find Hannigan and send him up to my office."

It was now dark outside. The traffic was heading out to the suburbs of Dublin. In his office, Raymond Mackin smiled contentedly at his reflection in the window. He enjoyed, in fact revelled, in the power that money had brought him. He thought of his father who, ten years ago, in order to evade the inland revenue, had abandoned his family and set up home with his secretary in Nerja, near Malaga. He was a partner with his brother in a shirt factory in the city centre. Mackin's mother was the daughter of a northside fruit merchant. There was a distinct record of madness in her family. A couple of years ago, she travelled to visit her elder sister in Texas. Her sister was a patient in the Dallas State Mental Hospital. Mackin presented his mother with a credit card at the airport.

After a couple of transatlantic calls, he proposed that she might like to stay on in Texas to nurse her sister back to health. Mackin purchased them a small apartment. Then he cancelled the credit card and his mother's return air ticket. He heard that she was now working as a waitress in a diner. Mackin had felt that at last she has found her true vocation.

Mackin sat behind his antique mahogany desk. He was not unduly worried. Indeed, he was at one with the fact that he had built his financial empire upon the shattered careers and lives of his employees, clients and friends.

Mackin often claimed, "This is my jungle and if you cannot feed or nurture me then you have no right to be here."

The desk calendar declared:

The best minds of this generation were destroyed by madness.

There was a knock on the door.

"Come in!" Mackin roared. He enjoyed frightening young Bernard Hannigan. "Well, how was your day," Mackin asked cynically. "Did you purchase the Pacific shares?"

"Yes," replied Hannigan feebly.

"Well, are the facts going to remain a secret or are you going to enlighten me?"

"I purchased one hundred and fifty thousand shares at the price limit you set of ninety-seven pence and recorded the transactions in your personal account."

Mackin looked at his computer screen. The Dublin market was strong. There was plenty of activity on the exchange.

"Come here!" Mackin pointed to the screen. "There are the Pacific shares that you purchased this morning. They are being offered for sale at the moment for ninety-nine pence, but the dealers are only bidding ninety-seven pence. Instruct Ronan at the exchange to buy three thousand at ninety-nine pence. Tell him that you have just received word from South Africa that Pacific have ordered a very expensive diamond drill head and that an investment this large indicates that they have, as rumoured, struck oil."

Hannigan rang through to the exchange and passed on Mackin's buy order, then returned to watch the computer screen. As his eyes focused on the screen, there was a flurry of excitement on the floor of the stock exchange as Ronan purchased the shares. Minutes later, this activity reflected in the altered image on the computer.

Above Mackin's nicotined index finger, the computer now recorded that Pacific were being offered at one pound and four pence and that the dealers were bidding one pound and two pence. Mackin was skilfully working the market and increasing the value of his shares. In minutes, he had increased the value of his shares by five pence per share.

"Call Ronan again. Tell him to make two further buys of two thousand shares, the first at one pound and four pence, the second twenty minutes later at one pound seven pence. Tell him the market must close tonight in excess of one pound seven pence."

Mackin pulled and opened a file from his desk drawer. He then tapped a few numbers on his telephone keyboard.

"Hello, is that Barrett and Company? This is Raymond Mackin. I would like to speak to Chris."

Mackin turned to Hannigan who was standing obediently and nervously at his shoulder.

"We have created a market for our shares. Now we must convince some of our clients that they should purchase them at the inflated price," Mackin chuckled.

"Chris, Raymond Mackin here. I have something that will interest you. There is a whisper that Pacific are about to announce a very significant oil find. Word around the exchange is that this morning their finance director ordered a one million pound diamond drill head from a South African drilling company. The market has responded in the last hour by rising from ninety-seven pence to one pound seven pence. I have just picked up a small block of fifty thousand on the London exchange at one pound five pence. I thought that, as one of our special clients, you should be given first option. Hold on a second, Chris. Something is flashing on the computer. Pacific … are … offered now at one pound ten pence. Maybe I should keep them for myself?"

Within ten minutes, Mackin had successfully off-loaded the Pacific shares at a profit of in excess of thirteen thousand pounds. Hannigan was disconcerted. What Mackin was doing was highly illegal. He was buying shares, placing them in his own account, creating a false market, then selling the shares at a profit to his own clients.

"Now Mr. Hannigan, that's what I call a good return for an hour's work! You are as big a criminal now as your old man. What will your mammy say?"

Hannigan's father, like Mackin's, had moved to Spain in the early eighties. He had been involved in an insurance swindle. There were few companies in the financial world that would employ Bernard Hannigan and Mackin knew this and exploited it. Hannigan, as a result, despised Mackin and the power he exerted over him. He was helpless and, through his naiveté, was an accessory to nearly all the business frauds Mackin had perpetrated. He contented himself, though, in the knowledge that a Sunday newspaper, with his help, was about to break a story on Mackin.

"What will I do with the seven thousand shares Ronan bought?" Hannigan enquired.

Mackin thought for a moment then smiled.

"Credit them to the account of Dr. Joan Curry and tell Noreen I want to see her ... now!"

આ આ આ

Noreen Harte was a twenty-five-year-old woman who had a singular mission in life. The morning she abandoned her parents' council house in Drimnagh and moved into her flat in Rathmines, she entered Peter Marks in Grafton Street and had her mousy, shoulder-length brown hair died blonde. She was determined not to end up like her mother, working as a part-time cleaning lady in an accountant's office with a husband who spent his life within the eternal triangle of the labour exchange, pub and bookies. Noreen was not the brightest girl in her class, but over the years, through a great deal of hard work, had amassed enough points in school to study accountancy.

The night Raymond Mackin walked into the Portobello, she knew she had her man. She found his arrogance and aura of self-importance comical. He stood at the bar flashing his gold credit cards wanting everyone to know who and what he was.

"A real man does not drink a gin and tonic!" Noreen joked with her friend.

Mackin considered himself a ladies' man and, as such, was an easy prey for Noreen. He never realised he could be cleverly manipulated by the female species he so openly mocked and suppressed. Over the following weeks, Noreen exercised the full power of her charm and guile on a willing and strangely naive Raymond Mackin. She escorted the childlike Mackin to all the major eateries and clubs. She even spent a weekend on his yacht, sailing around the Isle of Wight. She was subsequently rewarded with the position of trainee accountant. Mackin was not put off by the fact that Noreen was likely to fail her exams. In fact, he rewarded her by presenting her with a brand new white Honda Civic as a company car.

"She works a great deal of overtime and it's cheaper than paying for taxis," reasoned Mackin when questioned at a subsequent board meeting.

Noreen rewarded Mackin's confidence and support by crashing the car and carefully obscuring his fraudulent dealings.

In many ways, Noreen and Mackin were well suited. They were both cold and deliberate. Noreen had often met Mackin's vivacious wife, Veronica, socially. Indeed, once she and Raymond sailed to the Isle of Man to lodge some money to an account in the Bank of Ireland. Veronica flew in unexpectedly with their son as a surprise. It was that weekend that Veronica pieced together all the warnings her friends had given her. Mackin reacted angrily on his return by burning her cheque book and credit cards. While he no longer loved his wife, he was deeply aware that a divorce would be a costly affair. He found it infinitely cheaper to bankroll Veronica's passion for horses, so he bought her a new Land Rover Discovery.

Back in his office, Mackin dialled his home number. There was no answer.

Veronica and Raymond were married eighteen years now. At first, he had been infatuated and somewhat humbled by Veronica's interest in him. She was a successful model when they first met. He had problems coming to terms with the attention afforded her when they were out. People considered her infinitely more interesting than him. Mackin was only of novelty value. He was never comfortable with the fact that, in essence, Veronica was supporting him. Their relationship was tempestuous. Indeed, it almost ceased when Veronica announced that she was pregnant. Children at this juncture were not on Mackin's agenda. He demanded that the child be made available for adoption. Over the following years, Mackin was responsible for many acts of mental and physical cruelty, including damning his son, born with a congenital heart problem, to a life of emotional neglect — a more subtle form of child abuse. As he stood in Mount Carmel nursing home looking into the incubator at the scrawny and shrivelled pre-mature baby with black and blue blotches on his body, he turned to Veronica and said,

"This child will not be capable of doing any of the things that a father looks forward to enjoying with his son. Surely nothing this pathetic can survive." Mackin's remark was in hope rather than fear. Veronica never forgave him.

"Bernard said you wanted to see me?" Noreen enquired.

"Yes. Monday is the end of the month's account. Hannigan has contract notes for a few deals I processed today. I want the contract notes sent out this evening and couriers sent on Monday morning to collect payment. I also want you to ring Glackin, Strahan & O'Donnell solicitors and have them issue proceedings against Dr. Joan Curry for the amount outstanding on her account."

The phone rang. It was the receptionist.

"It's your wife, Mr. Mackin."

Mackin covered the mouthpiece of the phone. Noreen walked towards the door.

"You'd better give me the key to the apartment," he said. "You will be working late. I will wait for you in the Queen's."

"Raymond ... Raymond, are you there?" It was Veronica. What is wrong with her now? Mackin thought.

"Raymond, I have just spoken to the doctor. I am on a public phone." Veronica whispered now, "please can you come over to the hospital. I need to see you."

"I'm at a meeting right now. I will try and drop in later."

An hour later, finding the weekend traffic heading out of the city building into a jam, Mackin reluctantly turned the car and headed for the hospital. He found Veronica sitting on his son's bed. She was stroking his forehead. For the first time Mackin considered that his son might die.

Later, as he drove home, he decided that he owed it to the boy to at least determine if he was receiving the best possible treatment. The traffic had eased now. Indeed, it flowed smoothly. On the by-pass near Cabinteely, however, there was a hold-up. He wondered what had caused it. Mackin looked at the car clock. Moments later, he saw the crashed BMW Coupe and the swirling lights of a speeding ambulance. It was after nine. Noreen will be waiting in the Queen's. He dialled his car phone.

CHAPTER 3

Dan Kinsella closed the door of his council house and stepped out into the night chill. He was in his late forties, a heavy set man with a square face. His eyes were slow and intent, his mouth deeply carved beneath a drooping moustache. He had lived in Cornelscourt for almost thirty years now. Looking up the hill, he regarded with disdain the lights in the modern housing estates.

When they first arrived, full of hope, St. Brigid's Park looked out over rolling hills all the way to Stepaside. Old Mick Cunningham cleared the storm drains with a shovel he carried like a rifle over his shoulder. In his other hand, he clutched the reins of an enormous draft horse. The wooden council cart rattled behind them, the mugs and pots swinging from side to side. There was the smell of Mrs. Cox's greenhouse tomatoes, the sight of Charlie, the postman, spending his afternoons arguing politics in the glass house with Delia Cox. Dan worked with Charlie in the post office in Foxrock village. Charlie was one of the great characters who had managed the shortest postal round in Dublin. On a good day, Charlie would arrive at the post office at six thirty a.m.. After sorting his letters, he would set off down Westminster Road on his bicycle. Half an hour later, he would wheel the bike across the Bray Road to the parochial house. At nine thirty, he would finish in Cornelscourt.

Dan noted that the majestic Dublin mountains were no longer visible. They were now clouded in smoke and concrete. His wife, Deirdre, lay in the cemetery in Deansgrange. Their life had been frugal, but full of happiness. Deirdre could not bear children, so eighteen years ago they adopted Shane. Dan was glad that Deirdre had lived long enough to see Shane grow into a fine, handsome young man with a strength of character and resolve that would make any parent proud. Only that week, Shane had received word that he had been accepted by the Royal College of Surgeons to study medicine. He was probably down in the Horse & Hound now, celebrating with his friends.

"How are you, Pat?" Dan enquired of an elderly lady making her way back from the snug in the Magic Carpet.

"I'm not well, Mr. Kinsella. I don't think I am long for this world."

Pat was another great character from St. Bridgid's Park. She always seemed old to Dan. For as long as he could remember she had had grey hair, worn the same camel coat and joked that she was sick. Every night she sat alone in the snug, wrapped around the radiator and cradling a glass of Paddy. She would never admit that it was whiskey, though.

"Another glass of ginger ale please, Eamonn!"

Tonight, she was escorted by old Jimmy, the church sacristan. Poor Jimmy was given a hard time by the gang that used to play football in the car park behind Foxrock church. One summer's day, while Jimmy was weeding a flower bed, Dan slipped into the sacristy and spiked the altar wine with vodka. They always suspected that Jimmy enjoyed the sweet altar wine and the following morning, before seven o'clock mass, their suspicions were all but confirmed when the parish priest apprehended Jimmy mowing the car park with a lawnmower.

Dan headed out of St. Bridgid's Park and made towards Dunnes Stores. In the distance, he heard an ambulance siren. Since Deirdre had died, he had given up cigarettes. He walked every night along the Bray Road to Cabinteely, then up Brennanstown Road to Carrickmines Cross and back down Cornelscourt Hill.

Deirdre's death had rocked him to his foundations. He vowed the day she died that he would upgrade his Voluntary Health Insurance payments to Private so that if anything should happen to Shane he would receive the best possible treatment. Deep in his sub-conscious, Dan blamed himself for the fact that Deirdre's illness was not detected sooner.

"If she had been a private patient, she would have seen the specialist sooner," Dan argued as he relived the day Dr. Martin had informed him of the seriousness of Deirdre's illness. Dan thought that it was only tonsillitis.

"Dan, I would like to speak to you," Dr. Martin had whispered as the nurses pulled the screen around Deirdre's bed. "Prepare yourself. There is something that both you and Shane have to face."

Dr. Martin regarded Dan compassionately. "She has cancer, cancer of the throat. I have not told her and I do not believe she should be told either."

Dan swallowed and stared at Dr. Martin. He had not really understood the gravity of what the doctor had just told him.

"Cancer of the throat? I do not understand, doctor."

"There is no easy way to say this, Dan ... There is no possible doubt. Believe me when I say I wish there was. I am afraid it is in the final stages. There is no evidence that, even if it had been diagnosed sooner, we could have done any more. All we can do is relieve her suffering. She will be dead, I fear within, three months."

"Three months?" Dan queried.

"At the outside. The growth is out of control now. I feel that it would actually be a blessing for her if she died tonight."

"Can you not operate? All I hear on all those damn medical programmes is the great advancements you are making in medicine. Surely you can try something?"

"I am sincerely sorry, Dan. There is nothing modern medicine can do for Deirdre now. You can, however, do something. Pray for a peaceful and painless death." ·

As the months passed, Deirdre quickly faded from a vibrant, outwardly healthy woman with hope to a pitiful shadow of the woman Dan had known and loved. He cherished every lucid moment spent with her. As time went on and as the level of morphine was increased, these special moments were fewer.

One afternoon, they stood at an open window overlooking the hospital garden. Dan stood behind, supporting Deirdre. As he buried his face in her lifeless chestnut-coloured hair, Dan considered for one awful moment lifting Deirdre and hurling her to the concrete path below. It would be crime, but it would release her from her drug-induced nightmare. He wondered what agonies she bore, silently and bravely.

Shane, like Dan, would sit for hours stroking his mother's hand. Her eyes were lonely and frightened, his moist and indelibly tear-stained. Finally, the great dosages of morphine obliterated her mind and all that remained was a wizened alien body. For hours she lay there, staring blankly at Dan and Shane. There was no hope now. They prayed fervently that her soul be taken.

The following night, as Dan sat looking at Deirdre slipping in and out of consciousness, he came to the realisation that the woman he had married was no longer in the room with him. The emaciated body that lay in the bed opposite was no longer of this world. The Deirdre he knew and loved was long gone. It suddenly became all too much for Dan.

"If there is a God above, why have you given this good woman so much pain and hardship to bear? I plead with you to take her soul, release her from her suffering, let her die. Please … please let it end!"

The nurses came running from their station. Dr. Martin and Shane were close behind. They had arrived, not to console Dan, but to see to Deirdre. Dr. Martin checked her pulse, then looked at Dan and Shane.

"The Lord has answered your plea, Dan. Deirdre has finally joined him."

Dan was almost fifty-years-old, five foot nine and of stocky build. His thick grey hair has been worn long with a fringe since he was a teenager. He always dressed in a neat pair of slacks, a patterned jumper and a white shirt and tie. When he was younger, he did a lot of amateur wrestling with Gerry Martina in the national stadium. Many who encountered him considered him a gentleman with a quick wit and a pleasant nature. The few who crossed him witnessed a man with a ferocious passion and strength. Despite the fact that Deirdre could not bear children, Dan always considered Shane to be nobody else's son other than his own. He was immensely fortified by the fact that Shane had appeared to inherit his sense of morality, values and fair play. Dan owed money to nobody and preached that if you could not afford something then you were not meant to have it.

As Dan came into Cabinteely, he saw a crowd gathered outside the Horse & Hound and the flashing lights of the ambulance siren he had heard earlier. As he came closer to the accident, the ambulance pulled away with a squeal of tyres. Dan stopped for a moment to look at the crashed B.M.W. being loaded onto the recovery truck.

"Some people are morbid," Dan thought as he headed up Brennanstown Road.

"Dan Kinsella!" a voice bellowed from behind. Dan turned. It was the local garda sergeant.

"Can you come into the station for a moment?"

"I did not see anything, sergeant. I have only arrived now."

In the speeding squad car on the way to the Mater Hospital, a young garda explained to Dan how the accident happened.

"Don't worry, sir. I'm sure he will be all right. Your son was very lucky. A young woman doctor followed the ambulance from the by-pass and has travelled with Shane to the hospital."

CHAPTER 4

The driver, his forehead wet with nervous perspiration, radioed ahead. The ambulance sped towards the city centre, streaking past the menace of bicycles, buses and lorry trailers. At White's Cross, the lights began to turn from green to red. The siren wailed loudly and the traffic pulled over. The ambulance driver found a gap and accelerated on to Stillorgan.

Something fell from the injured man's pocket as the ambulance swung from side to side, threading its way through the city centre traffic. Dr. Curry picked it up. It was a wallet. She handed it to the ambulance man. Dr. Curry looked at the young patient. His long hair was matted in dried blood and his face was a mass of pulped flesh. His blood pressure was low, his respiratory pattern normal. He began to gag. Dr. Curry checked that his air passage was clear then replaced the nasal oxygen. He started to convulse. Dr. Curry observed the precise manner in which the minor seizure proceeded. The young man's eyes and head turned distinctly to the right. Her initial prognosis had been that the injuries were centred in the chest and abdomen with possible internal bleeding. Dr. Curry now feared that the symptoms indicated a frontal lobe seizure on the left side of the brain. Suddenly, the boy's athletic body stiffened and began to jerk rhythmically, his hand first, then his arm, then his entire body. The spasm was violent. Dr. Curry, with the boy's head cradled in her arms, fought to keep his airway clear. Both she and the startled ambulance man watched in horror as the tormented young man's seizure-racked body twisted and turned involuntarily.

As swiftly as the spasm began, it subsided. Dr. Curry looked out the side window of the ambulance. They were

34

turning off Dorset Street and approaching the hospital. The doors of the ambulance opened and the patient was removed. Dr. Curry noticed an organ donor card on the floor of the ambulance. It must have fallen out of the wallet, she reasoned. There, staring up from the flip side of the donor card, was a student identity card, on it the smiling face of a handsome, carefree young man.

Shane Kinsella. 3 St. Bridgid's Park, Cornelscourt.
Born 7-10-77

As Shane was wheeled into casualty on the gurney, a well-oiled machine swung into action. Doctors and nurses moved with purpose in all directions. A miscellany of local and foreign accents spiralled from the focal point — Shane's crumpled body. Dr. Curry spoke earnestly with the duty doctor, Mr. Brennan, while he gently removed Shane's neck brace. Dr. Curry cut away Shane's blood-soaked clothes. A nurse began to connect Shane up to a life support machine. A porter wheeled in x-ray equipment and handed out the protective vests. A nurse cleaned a deep gash in Shane's forehead and gently removed the dried blood and grit from his deformed and crushed face. Shane, Dr. Curry thought, was only barely recognisable as the young man on the student identity card.

"I'm afraid, Dr. Curry, that we must assume the worst." Dr. Brennan's tone was grave."Nurse, stop taking blood! Stand back, people. I want this young man's neck, spine, chest and pelvic areas x-rayed."

While Shane was being x-rayed, Dr. Brennan and Dr. Curry carefully examined his swollen abdomen. The accomplished surgeons moved swiftly and skilfully.

"Nurse, I concur with Dr. Curry. Immediate surgical intervention is required. This young man is bleeding internally."

While Dr. Brennan cut an opening in Shane's abdomen and inserted a tube to drain blood from the cavity, Dr. Curry was bombarded with visions of Declan's battered body at the bottom of the ravine in Peru, Raymond Mackin sarcastically enquiring, "Would you like me to buy you a few more shares?" and young James in the private room above.

As they waited to view the x-rays, casualty became strangely silent for a moment. All that could be heard was the hiss and click of the ventilator and the constant murmur emanating from the waiting room. Dr. Brennan placed the x-rays in the viewing box and nervously stroked his chin with his thumb and forefinger. He shook his head from side to side, then spoke to Dr. Curry.

"This young man is in a poor way. To be honest, with these injuries he should be dead. Indeed, if the truth be known, in my opinion he would be better off dead. We must do a C.T. scan immediately. Nurse, I will call the radiologist. Have Mr. ...," Dr. Brennan looked at Shane's chart, "Kinsella taken for an immediate C.T. scan!"

Dr. Brennan turned to Dr. Curry.

"You look tired, Joan. Why don't you go home and get some rest. I will call you if there are any developments."

Dr. Curry walked from casualty, took the lift to the first floor and looked in on James. She spoke to his distressed mother, then went home. Before she left the hospital, she wrote two letters — one to the stock exchange, the other to her solicitor.

ୟ ୟ ୟ

Back in Cabinteely, outside the garda station, an angry crowd had gathered. The old pebble-dashed station, originally a modest terraced council house, was under siege

36

by an angry mob. Inside, two young boys, their faces pale and blank, were being interrogated by an angry garda. The boys sat passively behind a table, their arms folded in defiance. Outside in the reception area, a young worried-looking garda was calling Deansgrange station looking for back up.

"Do you realise that you killed a man tonight?" the sergeant asked the younger boy. "Are you proud of yourself? What will your mother think? What will your father think? They will love to introduce their murdering son to the neighbours! Maybe they don't care. Is that it then? … Do you care?"

Another garda came from behind the boy and flicked ash from a lighted cigarette down the back of his shirt collar.

"If you won't talk to us, maybe then you'd rather speak to the men outside?"

The garda sergeant was infuriated, but he recognised the signs: the blank vacant look and clothes riddled in cigarette burns. These young boys were on drugs.

"Garda Flynn, release the boys without charge!"

The burly garda pulled the boys roughly to their feet and dragged them into the reception area.

"John Mannion," the youngest boy offered.

"What's that?" The sergeant bellowed. "Did one of you scum say something?"

"I will tell yis if yis don't ring me ma. Right?"

"Right. Go on then!"

"John Mannion! And his name is Kevin Costello. We legged it from St. Lawrence's earlier. We didn't mean to kill the lad, but he shouldn't have been crossing the road anyway!"

Garda Flynn pushed the boys back into the interrogation room.

37

An hour later, as the boys were beginning to break under the pressure exerted by the gardai, a harsh woman's voice could be clearly heard above the crowd at the front of the station.

"Get out of my way! Don't yis push me. Let me through!"

The crowd moved back to allow the woman to approach the front door of the station. She climbed the steps, then turned to face the angry crowd.

"Whatever about you shower of bowsies, I'll murder him when I get me hands on him!"

A marked garda van and a two squad cars pulled up at the traffic lights. Twenty gardai set about swiftly and efficiently clearing up the crowd outside the station.

"You promised you wouldn't ring me ma!"

"I didn't ... I rang your da!" the sergeant laughed loudly. "Garda Flynn, let the woman in."

Rhona Mannion lived in Ballyfermot and was forty-five years old. Her husband, three years her junior, had no control over his three sons, of whom John was the youngest. The older boys were in Mountjoy for aggravated burglary. Like John, they were not hardened criminals. They were just easily motivated and led by young men like Costello. John, his angelic face and brain numbed by solvents and fear, was himself a father. His girlfriend, Rosemary, had given birth to a baby boy two months ago.

Rhona ran her fingers through her short, greasy, peroxide blonde hair and lit a cigarette. She was adamant that John would not follow in his brother's footsteps, but as the sergeant detailed the horrors of what had happened earlier, she came to the cold realisation that, in one night, her third and youngest son John had emulated his brothers.

CHAPTER 5

Mackin sat alone in the Queen's in Dalkey. It was almost ten o'clock. Noreen hadn't arrived. He had grown tired of her. All the little things about her that had once excited him now annoyed him. He had sold the apartment in a gesture of defiance. He knew that the move from the three bedroom penthouse apartment on Killiney Hill to the one bedroom in Seaview, which overlooked the main street in Sandycove, would upset Noreen. He did not care. It was a calculated move.

"This is not a luxury apartment. It's an old folks home!" Noreen had roared at Mackin.

Mackin wanted to crush Noreen's resolve. He wanted her to terminate their volatile relationship. He was mindful that, should it end any way other than amicably, Noreen, armed with the wealth of knowledge she had garnered from his fraudulent dealings, could cause him great embarrassment. The only comfort was that she had knowingly supported and profited from his deceits. She was a fiery, working class woman with an indomitable determination, something that Mackin found impossible to harness at times. He felt sure that she was as calculated as he was. Recently, she'd been drinking more and was noticeably unpredictable and vigilant with him, especially after she had been out with her friends. Mackin was certain that they were fuelling her growing dissatisfaction.

At ten-thirty, Noreen strode into the Queen's. She was drunk and dressed to attract attention. This annoyed Mackin as he chose to pass unnoticed. Noreen had done this purposely as an act of defiance.

"Why are you dressed like that? You look like a whore!" Mackin demanded.

"Would sir like me to change into in a long black dress and woollen shawl like all the other old women in the home I'm staying in?"

Noreen was fired with rocket fuel. Mackin ordered drinks. Before they arrived, Noreen stood.

"I'm hungry. I want something to eat," she declared.

The waiter brought a gin and tonic for Mackin and a vodka and orange for Noreen. She downed her drink in one gulp.

"I'm starving. I want to eat," Noreen repeated loudly. The people at the next table turned. Mackin glared at them.

"Do you hear me? I would like to eat now! Maybe I should call that man in Athlone you sold your Pacific shares to today. He may appreciate me more! What was his name? Barrett ... yes, Chris Barrett."

Mackin downed his gin and tonic and led Noreen to the Al Minar restaurant. He requested a quiet table. She ordered a bottle of white wine. He remained silent, contemplative. She was like a coiled spring. She frightened him.

"Ah, will you look who it is! My esteemed cousin, the high-flying stockbroker, slumming it in a common Indian restaurant. Are you not on your luxury yacht this weekend? Maybe it's tied up in the harbour below? You must introduce me to this beautiful young woman. Let me guess. She is a friend of your wife's, looking for spiritual or maybe even financial support no doubt? Ha ha."

"My name is Noreen. I am a ... a colleague of Mr. Mackin!" She offered the man her hand, enjoying Raymond Mackin's embarrassment.

"Madame, allow me to introduce myself. I am John Mackin. This is my wife, Heather. Unfortunately, this piece of dirt is my first cousin. He is just like his father. He probably told you that his old man emigrated to Spain due to ill health. Well, the truth is ..."

Raymond Mackin was cornered and smiled nervously. Noreen laughed. The proprietor observed curiously.

"Two months ago, Raymond rang and told me of an entertainment company coming to the market in the U.K. He said that he had a friend in the stockbroking company backing the floatation and could buy the shares at the time for five pence each. 'I will put you in for twenty grand's worth,' he told me on the phone. 'It won't cost you a penny. I will buy, then sell the shares at a premium as soon as they hit the market.'"

John Mackin was shouting now.

"'I will also get Noreen to set up a false account for you,' he told me. 'That way, the tax man won't be able to trace you.' Hold on ... Noreen? ... Noreen? That name is familiar."

The head waiter intervened and led John Mackin to the door of the restaurant. His wife remained at the table staring directly at Mackin. She spoke in a cultured accent.

"You have ruined us. We did not have twenty thousand pounds to, as you say, speculate with. This afternoon, the bank manager informed us that we must sell our house to repay the debt you forced upon us. It was going to be so easy. You told John that there was no risk whatsoever. You would simply sell the shares before payment was due.

"'Don't worry!' John told me, 'Raymond says that he will sell the shares within the account.' Good old cousin Raymond, I thought! But you did nothing. Now the shares are worthless ... just like you. I wonder how you sleep at night in your big house in Stepaside. It's a lonely area. I wouldn't live up there — too many odd people roaming the mountains at night-time. You could be murdered in your bed and nobody would even know!

"Beware, Mr. Mackin. The city that nurtures you today could strangle you tomorrow. A word of warning! You once said that Dublin was your orchard and that you had reached out and gathered the fruit from its branches and that the same fruit is there for everyone, that is if they are not afraid to climb the ladder. You have chosen to go to war, but you have made an elementary mistake. Before you go into battle, you must always establish the strengths and weaknesses of your enemy You established the weak link with John. Now meet the strength."

Heather now leaned on the table and placed her face close to Mackin's. She spoke in a harsh Dublin accent.

"I love John. I am all the things that he wants me to be. At this moment, more than anything, he needs me to be strong. Mr. Mackin, the fruit in your orchard is diseased. My advise to you is don't park your car in a back street. Don't even get out of it at night to close your gates. Not tonight, not ever. I am going to see to it that your ladder is taken away."

Heather turned and left the restaurant. Mackin was ashen-faced. The young Indian waiter came to the table and began to pour the wine.

"Get me a brandy!" Mackin demanded.

"I am sorry, sir, but we do not have a full licence."

"Listen to me, you damn fool!" Mackin swung around, his eyes mad, his temple pulsing and the side of his neck palpitating. "You serve Irish coffees, don't you? ... Well don't you?"

"Yes, sir." The young waiter's eyes darted around the restaurant looking for assistance.

"Put the brandy in the glass. Do you understand?"

The waiter nodded.

"And forget to pour in the coffee and cream!"

Mackin was incensed. He sat in silence, his eyes still wild. After awhile, he raised his head and spoke calmly.

"I had lunch with Glanville, the regulation manager in

the stock exchange, today. Out of the blue he called and suggested that we meet. He told me that he had received an anonymous letter detailing a number of so-called fraudulent transactions that had allegedly been carried out by R.M. & P.. Would you have any idea who may have sent this letter? Perhaps, may I suggest that it could be down to something simple, like a woman scorned?"

As Mackin spoke, Noreen ran her fingers through her long blond hair. She could see that Mackin was worried.

"Wait a minute!" Noreen interrupted. "I am merely a young, infatuated trainee accountant carrying out instructions from the managing director. What would I know?"

Mackin fidgeted nervously. As a student, soon after his father's clothing company had been wound up, he had encountered the criminal underworld in a pub opposite the Four Courts in Dublin. A man his father left owing money to approached him in the toilets and vowed that some day he would exact retribution. Mackin could never forget the man's angry face and powerful disposition, but he had completely forgotten about the incident until eighteen months ago when the man had called to his office.

"Mr. Mackin," he had said, "you may remember that we spoke some years ago when your father decided to leave the country with funds belonging to an organisation I represent. Well, I said then that there would be reprisals. I have been ordered to instruct you to carry out a number financial transactions on our behalf."

The man who spoke to Mackin was an arms dealer. He was a powerful man who bought and sold arms from Belfast to Beirut. The organisation, as he described it, knew little about the workings of the stock market, only that it provided a mechanism for them to convert sterling into punts and subsequently bring funds into the country.

"How much does Glanville know?" Noreen queried.

"I don't know."

Noreen noted that Mackin now had the appearance of a frightened child. She almost reached out to console him. She was annoyed with her lack of resolve.

"The vice is beginning to tighten, Mr. Mackin."

Noreen now spoke venomously.

"If the stock exchange carry out an investigation, they will find that not alone did you disadvantage clients for your own gain, but you have also broken the exchange laws and conspired to deceive the inland revenue." Noreen laughed loudly, lit a cigarette and blew the smoke in Mackin's face then continued, "How will the organisation react when they discover that their funds have been intercepted by the fraud squad? You are a fool. They offered you the opportunity to repay your father's debt and you rewarded that trust by relieving them of eighteen thousand pounds on a single deal."

Without averting her gaze, Noreen removed a hair tie from her handbag and, while gathering her hair in a pony tail, she stood up and declared, "I would not like to be you. If you're lucky, you'll end up back where your family started — pushing fruit barrows around Moore Street."

Mackin remained seated as Noreen calmly walked from the restaurant. He finished his brandy and meal, then drove his old Mercedes to Dun Laoghaire and walked along the pier. Young couples walked hand in hand oblivious to the cold. He was alone.

¿♠ ¿♠ ¿♠

James lay awake, tossing and turning on the bed. His appearance was haggard. His eyes were grey and lifeless. Veronica was asleep in the chair. Her eyes were green and warm. Her long fair hair endowed her with a softness that

44

was decidedly feminine. She sensed a presence in the room and turned. Her husband was framed in the doorway. She stared at Mackin through dazed and fearful eyes.

"Are you all right, James?" Veronica was concerned.

James kicked back the bed covers. Mackin noted that his son's face was gaunt, but his legs and ankles were swollen. He was still retaining fluid. James attempted to speak but a fountain of bile gushed from his mouth.

"I'm sorry, dad! I can't help it! I wish I was ..."

James's face suddenly winced, his head went back and his eyes danced around the ceiling.

"Are you all right, James? What's wrong?"

Veronica panicked. She ran to the door looking for a nurse. Mackin stood transfixed and utterly useless.

"How do you feel?" he enquired.

"I feel funny. Hot flushes. My back aches. I can't see. Everything is in black and white. Silhouetted. Mum, am I dying? Everything is a haze."

James began to vomit again. Two nurses arrived. One reassured Veronica, but the other's eyes told her that James was having a heart attack.

"There is nothing you can do, Mrs. Mackin," the nurse reasoned. "I have called Dr. Curry. She is on her way."

Mackin stood behind his wife. She looked at him.

"You smell of cheap perfume," Veronica said.

CHAPTER 6

Dan sat alone in the casualty department. Everything seemed unreal. He observed that almost all the injuries being dealt with that night were drink related. A young man, his back a mass of tiny glass splinters, was wheeled in. He had been at a traditional music session in a city centre bar. He stood on a table to get a better view. A girl in front of him was pushed back against the table on which he was standing. He lost his balance and fell backwards onto another table laden with empty glasses. Not long after him, another teenager was wheeled in. He had fallen off the back of a high-powered motorbike and had been run over by a car. They feared that his back was broken. An old man, who had fallen down the stairs of his house with a bottle of whiskey in his hand, was having his wrist stitched and bandaged. A young man who had stolen a car and subsequently crashed it seriously, injuring his girlfriend, sat on the floor, his head securely buried in his hands.

Dan stood and walked towards the curtain which divided the waiting room from the casualty department. There were nurses and doctors running to and fro in feverish activity. He could see a frightened middle-aged woman, her arm in a sling, sitting on a bed and peering back through the curtain at him. The ailing woman with unseeing eyes looked straight through Dan. A plump red-haired nurse guided a mentally retarded girl who had been brought in earlier. She had accidentally cut her wrist with a Stanley knife. At the far end of the emergency room, a doctor spoke to an angelic little girl who had fallen into a bath filled with scalding water. Dan turned away as the doctor gave the screaming child a pain-relieving injection and began to cut away her tender outer layer of damaged skin. The child's body was red, raw and weeping. What skin remained was shrivelled and dangled like string. A distraught woman Dan took to be the child's mother paced up and down the waiting room with an ambulance man comforting her.

A young Indian doctor walked towards Dan. He was complaining to a nurse that he had already worked sixty-five hours that week and had just been put on stand-by for the weekend. The nurse pointed to Dan. The doctor led Dan away from the curtain into a corner.

"Mr. Kinsella, they have taken Shane up to have a C.T. scan. From there, he will be taken back to intensive care."

"How is he doctor?" Dan asked quietly.

"Shane's condition is stable at the moment, but we still have a lot of tests to run before Dr. Curry can make a diagnosis. The best thing you can do, Mr. Kinsella, is go home and try to get some rest. We have your phone number if there are any developments. We will call you."

"Doctor, you did not answer my question. How is Shane? Is he ... is he going to ... to die?"

"Mr. Kinsella," the doctor spoke in earnest, "Shane has been seriously injured. At the moment, he is unconscious. This in itself is not unusual. It is only the response of the body's defence mechanism to trauma. What we must determine is the extent of Shane's head injuries. The C.T. scan will provide this information. Mr. Kinsella, go home and come back in the morning. There is nothing you can do here, believe me."

Dan took the doctor's advice. He left the hospital and hailed a taxi. On the way home, he sat back in the dirty, four-door Toyota Carina and allowed his mind to wander back to the day that the local health nurse arrived with Shane. It was hard to describe the excitement and joy that day brought. Shane was a beautiful child with a kiss curl planted in the centre of his forehead. They were now a family. Dan vowed to provide for and protect them.

He remembered fondly his son's first day at the convent school. Shane had cried his lungs out, holding onto Mother Peter's hand while Dan walked down the long cinder path to the entrance gate. He did not dare to turn around. He remembered the school fancy dress party when Shane went dressed as a pirate and how he had returned distraught because his wooden sword was broken. At his first Holy Communion, Shane had been frightened that he would not be able to answer the Bishop's catechism question. Dan smiled as he remembered Shane standing in the hallway in his little white jumper and short trousers, his scarred, red, knobbly knees and holy medal shaking in terror. Then there was the ritual calling on aunts and uncles and the film afterwards: *A Long Day's Journey Into Night*. Shane had fallen asleep.

Dan thought of Shane's first pair of long grey trousers and how proud he had looked setting off to school on the bus. He was a grown-up. He recalled the long weekends they used to spend in a rented caravan in Brittas Bay. Shane would sit in a deserted sand dune in the middle of winter, the rain pouring down upon his sodden head and the crumbling sand castle. He remembered Shane playing football on Sunday mornings in the C.Y.C. under twelve's league. Dan would watch him sit eating his dinner, his bare legs caked in dried mud. Then there was Shane's trial with the Irish schoolboy football team in Ringsend, which had ended up in a brawl between the players and the spectators. He remembered the night that they had read in The Evening Press that Shane had been selected for the Irish team to play the Welsh schoolboys and he recalled the proud moment when he shook Shane's hand as he mounted the bus at Foxrock church. Shane was heading for the mailboat in

Dun Laoghaire on the first leg of his journey to Ninian Park in Cardiff. Dan thought of the endless days Shane had spent at his mother's grave, talking and praying.

Dan paid the taxi driver and went inside the house. At this moment he realised that, in twelve short months, his home had become merely a house. Walls which had once emanated happiness now radiated despair. He went into the kitchen and put on the kettle for a cup of tea. While he waited for it to boil, he went upstairs to run a bath. He walked into Shane's room. On the bedside table was an envelope addressed to Shane. It looked official. Dan read the contents, then placed the envelope in his coat pocket and went downstairs. There was a knock on the front door. Dan reluctantly opened it. Standing on the step was Father O'Connell, the local parish priest. Dan got a terrible shock.

"Oh father!" Dan moved back from the door. "Is Shane ..."

"Take it easy, Dan. This is only a social call. I have no word on Shane. I merely called to see if you are in need of support."

Fr. O'Connell walked directly into the kitchen. He produced a small bottle of Powers whiskey from his overcoat and made Dan a cup of strong coffee. He poured a good measure of whiskey into the cup. Dan spoke for almost an hour before he handed Fr. O'Connell the letter he had found in Shane's room. The elderly priest read the contents of the letter, then folded up the document and handed it back to Dan.

"There is nothing extraordinary in this, Dan."

"But why the secrecy, father?"

"Dan, you never made any secret of the fact that Shane was adopted. He is your son and will always be your son. But you are not his father and poor Deirdre was not his mother. Shane has an enquiring mind. He has the right to know, if he chooses, who his mother was and under what circumstances he was offered for adoption. I do not for a minute suspect that Shane wanted to deceive you. It appears that he merely requested his mother's address from the adoption agency."

"But, father, what do I do now? Shane is in intensive care! I must write to her, let her know. The woman is his mother! She has a right!"

Fr. O'Connell reflected for a few moments.

"Dan, I really don't think that would be a good idea. This is a very difficult time to approach Shane's mother. It is not fair to expose her to this hardship. I don't believe anything can be achieved. I will contact the convent tomorrow."

Fr. O'Connell wrote down the phone number and address of the adoption agency and the name of Shane's mother: Veronica Armitage.

CHAPTER 7

At six a.m., Joan eased herself out of bed, showered, dressed, drank a cup of lukewarm coffee and noted that there was a message on the answering machine. She pressed the play button.

"Hello. My name is Frederick Hanley. I am a reporter for The Business Post. I have been informed that you are encountering problems with a Dublin stockbroker. I would very much like to talk to you. Maybe when you get an opportunity you would return my call?"

Joan made a note of the number and headed into the hospital. She made her way to intensive care. The prognosis on Shane Kinsella was as she expected. She went to check on James, leaving instructions at the nurses' station that as soon as Dan Kinsella arrived, he was to be sent to her rooms. James was poorly. His attractive mother slept soundly. Dr. Curry decided to see her when she woke.

In her office, Dr. Curry reflected on the critical condition of her two young patients. There was a knock on the door.

"Come in!"

"Hello, Dr. Curry? My name is Dan Kinsella ... Shane's father."

"Come in, Mr. Kinsella. Please sit down."

Dr. Curry observed the broken disposition of the man sitting opposite her.

"Mr. Kinsella, I will be honest with you. Shane is in a coma. We expect that, if he should recover consciousness, he will be brain damaged, how badly at this time is difficult to determine."

Dan's fears became a reality. Dr. Curry moved to a viewing box and gestured for Dan to follow.

"This is a plate of Shane's brain from the C.T. scan we carried out last night." Dr. Curry traced the x-ray of Shane's brain with her finger until it rested upon a large grey area.

"I emphasise, Mr. Kinsella, that many victims of severe head injuries have the potential to make excellent recoveries from even the most serious brain damage. It is imperative, though, that we correctly interpret, assess and anticipate potential complications. Before I take you to see Shane in intensive care, you should be prepared to accept that his injuries are extensive and, visually, quite disturbing. The blow from the car has fractured and deformed his skull. I should add that the fact that his skull is fractured is worrying."

Dr. Curry led Dan to intensive care. He had never imagined that the head injuries could be so severe. He looked in absolute horror at the tormented body of his son then drew back, disbelieving. Shane's face and scalp were shaven and swollen to almost twice the normal size. He was a mass of bloody cuts and abrasions. The limp body lying semi-prone on the bed was unrecognisable as his son. Dan held Shane's cold, limp hand while he buried his head in the pillow and cried.

Dr. Curry checked Shane's blood pressure, then administered short stabs to his extremities. She checked his vital signs, respiration, blood pressure and pulse. She applied her stethoscope to the boy's heart and lungs. They were clear. She then examined his ribcage for contusions and palpated his abdomen, then his pelvis, spine and neck. A nurse injected medication. Dr. Curry spoke to her.

"Has he run any fevers?"

The nurse shook her head.

Dr. Curry used an otoscope to examine the boy's nose and ears for traces of blood or spinal fluid. With an ophthalmoscope, she focused on his bloodshot and deeply-veined eyes, looking for any sign of brain pressure or haemorrhage. The examination completed, she wrote her findings on his chart.

Dr. Curry came around and stood beside Dan. She grasped Shane's hand. It was limp and unresisting. His eyes were vague and uncertain. She smiled ruefully at Dan, trying to reassure him. His eyes were hollow and fixed.

"Mr. Kinsella, there is pressure on your son's brain caused by swelling and haemorrhage. The shift of brain tissue, should it continue, will raise the pressure, thus increasing the likelihood of irreversible damage. The normal brain maintains its blood supply within fairly narrow limits. The damaged brain that has lost the capacity to regulate its blood supply adds further complications."

Dr. Curry was aware that little, if any, of what she was saying was registering with Dan.

"Doctor," Dan confided, "Shane is all that I have. From what I gather, do you ...? Have you ...? Oh, I don't know what I am trying to say. Do you think ... Shane will live?"

Dr. Curry lifted Shane's hand and pinched his forearm. There was no response to this painful stimulation. She then removed a pencil-light torch from her pocket, opened one of Shane's eyelids and asked Dan to shine the bright light at one of his pupils. Again, there was no reaction. Dr. Curry took a deep breath. She knew that modern medicine could do little for Shane and that the best thing now would be divine intervention.

"Mr. Kinsella, apart from his horrific physical injuries, Shane is alive due to modern technology. He is in a coma with the absence of movement and sensation, relying on a machine to help him breathe. The fact that we have the skill to open a child's skull and explore his brain does not mean that we should rush into it. However, I consider it necessary to carry out an angiogram this morning. We will then operate to reduce the pressure and remove whatever damaged tissue and bone exists in his skull. The angiogram will determine the exact extent of Shane's injuries."

Dan Kinsella's face began to disintegrate. Dr. Curry continued.

"The next twenty-four hours are going to be very important. You will need to be both mentally and physically prepared. I strongly advise that you get some rest."

❧ ❧ ❧

As the daily routine of the hospital seemed to ebb and flow around her, Dr. Joan Curry made her way to the autopsy room. For the first time in her career, she questioned her resolve. The student doctors were already assembled and waiting for her.

Dr. Curry went to her locker, removed her white coat and thrust her arms into a gown. A young nurse stepped forward and tied the gown as she moved to a wash basin to scrub. The class watched as Dr. Curry put on her surgical gloves and read from a clipboard.

"Ladies and gentlemen, my name is Dr. Joan Curry. I am not a pathologist, as you know, but a heart surgeon. As pathologists, you will be considered by many as the doctor a patient only encounters after his death. You should, however, never underestimate the importance of your position. Remember, the dead teach the living. The pathologist toiling in the bowels of a hospital tests a patient's blood, identifies his diseases, determines whether a tumour is malignant or benign and, when all else fails, it is generally he who will make the final diagnosis."

Dr. Curry turned to the dead body of a middle-aged man laid out on a cold marble slab. Utilising the skill and speed of her long experience, Dr. Curry began the autopsy with two deep incisions which opened the patient from both shoulders to the bottom of his chest. She then tied off and cut the arteries. Within moments, Dr. Curry had removed the heart and lungs. After careful scrutiny, she asked the students to gather around.

"This man's medical history is that three years ago he suffered his first coronary attack. His second was earlier this week. First we will examine the coronary arteries."

Dr. Curry delicately opened the heart muscle arteries.

"Somewhere, we should find ... Yes, here it is — the area of thrombosis."

Pointing at the main branch of the left coronary artery with a scalpel, Dr. Curry exposed a pale half-inch clot.

"Now we will examine the heart itself!"

Dr. Curry laid the heart on a dissecting board and beckoned the hesitant students closer. She then sliced down the centre of the heart with a knife. and placed the two sections side by side. She continued.

"Here, do you see this area of scarring in the muscle?" Dr. Curry indicated some streaks of white fibrous tissue in the heart. "There's the evidence of the first coronary attack, an old infarct which has healed."

Dr. Curry paused to allow the students to inspect the heart.

"Here we have the signs of the latest attack in the left ventricle. Notice the area of pale ..."

The phone rang. A nurse answered and relayed the message.

"Dr. Curry, you're wanted on the second floor. It's an emergency!"

As Dr. Curry entered the private room on the second floor, a junior doctor lowered the arm of the elderly lady who had, as expected, finally submitted to the ravages of bowel cancer. The poor woman had endured more than she deserved. Death was a release. Dr. Curry looked across the room to the woman's son. No words were needed. A nurse methodically noted the time of death. She was in her third month of training and was still fascinated, but at the same time repulsed, with the finality of death.

All through her long illness, the woman had been solid emotionally and had met her fate without hysterics. Dr. Curry remembered the day when she had relayed the diagnosis and how the woman had at first been composed then broke down, acknowledging that the last barriers of hope had gone. As with Shane and James, Dr. Curry, although trained to be clinical and unemotional, was moved. At times as she grew older, she found it necessary to admit to herself that while a surface detachment was necessary it was, in essence, merely an act. She thought again of James and how, if he did not get a donor heart soon, he would never play football or swim again. His spirit would depart this world with few memories.

As she entered James's room, Dr. Curry regarded his mournful face and wondered what horrors he had endured. She vowed to find out who was responsible for the fractures that had appeared on the x-rays. She considered that, while mankind is now capable of making complex equipment that allows us to travel to the other end of the universe, we are helpless to understand what goes on in the mind of a single child.

"Dr. Curry, allow me to introduce my husband, Raymond."

James slept. His mother, Veronica, was seated on his bed. A man in a winged-back chair, with his back to Dr. Curry as he read The Irish Times, stood and turned towards her.

"Dr. Curry, this is my husband, Raymond … Mackin."

Dr. Curry was rooted to the spot. Mackin smiled and

offered a limp hand.

"I am glad to see James is in good care."

Mackin walked slowly and deliberately to the window before breaking the awkward silence.

"I am going to get a cup of coffee," he added as he left the room.

"I have to speak to you, Mrs. Mackin. Alone in my office." Dr. Curry's voice quivered noticeably as the colour drained from Veronica Mackin's cheeks. Noticing the woman's anguish, she added, "Don't worry. It has nothing to do with James's present condition."

In the sanctuary of the doctor's office, Veronica Mackin relaxed. She was a tall, slender woman, considerably younger than her husband. From her complexion, Dr. Curry deduced that she spent most of her time out of doors.

"Mrs. Mackin, I will come straight to the point. When I examined James the other day, I found some evidence of bruising. As a matter of course, as you know, I ordered x-rays, the results of which are here on my desk. Apart from the unexplained fractures that appear on the plates, I am of the opinion that your son exhibits a pattern of conduct that we generally find in cases of prolonged parental deprivation."

Veronica Mackin shook her head in confusion.

"It's not true. Simply not true. What fractures? Raymond loves James! Sometimes he may get annoyed with him, all fathers do, but he has never struck him, not in my presence anyway."

Dr. Curry placed an x-ray in the viewing box.

"Mrs. Mackin, this is an x-ray of James's left wrist. I suspect that it has been fractured within the last twelve months."

Without uttering a word, Dr. Curry placed another x-ray in the viewing box.

"Here is another x-ray, this time of James's right fibula, a bone in his leg. It has healed now. The injury was inflicted two or three years ago. These are not coincidences Mrs. Mackin."

Dr. Curry sat on her desk and looked directly into Veronica Mackin's eyes.

"There is also evidence of scar tissue on James's stomach, neck and groin."

Veronica Mackin sat back in the chair and closed her eyes. She cried. She had, of course, known for some time that Raymond had been physically abusing James. She recalled what he had said in the nursing home: "This child will not be capable of doing any of the things that a proud father looks forward to enjoying with his son. Surely nothing this pathetic can survive anyway."

Mackin considered his son to be an embarrassment. One night after James had taken a heavy fall at the local hunt in Redcross, Veronica had consoled James by saying that he had done his best. Raymond retorted, "When a man claims that he did his best, he is merely apologising for his failure." He had laughed. "If he is successful, there is no need for an explanation. If he fails no excuse will suffice."

Dr. Curry placed an arm around Veronica Mackin's shoulder.

"There is no professional confidentially in suspected child abuse cases. I have a moral and legal duty to report my findings. At the moment, though, the most important thing is to find a donor heart for James and I have no wish to add further complications."

Dr. Curry escorted Veronica back to James's room.

CHAPTER 8

Raymond Mackin, his Irish Times folded under his arm, took the lift down to the reception area of the hospital. He bought a packet of cigarettes. He was for the first time encountering a new emotion ... guilt. He had accepted that unless James received a donor heart he would, in all probability, die.

In the staff restaurant, Mackin queued behind two nurses. He guessed they had just come off duty.

"That poor Kinsella boy, the one in the coma. He is in a very bad way, isn't he?"

The other nurse sighed and poured a glass of milk.

"I have never seen anybody survive with such horrendous injuries!" she continued. "His back, neck and pelvis were broken. Did you see the x-rays? His head was crushed. If he lives, he will be severely brain damaged."

"The ambulance man," the other nurse interrupted, "said that he had been dragged for over one hundred yards under the car. The joy riders only stopped when they crashed into a traffic light. He said that a couple of lads coming out of the pub gave them a hiding. In fact, they would have been killed only the gardai intervened."

"Dr. Brennan told Dr. Curry that he should be dead. Indeed, he said that if the truth be known Shane Kinsella would be better off dead."

Mackin picked up a tray, selected a salad sandwich and poured a mug of black coffee. He sat alone in the corner reading the Times. At another table next to him, he noticed a middle-aged man leaning back in his chair. His eyes were closed. He was in deep contemplation.

Mackin's mobile phone rang. He pulled up the aerial and flicked open the mouthpiece.

"Raymond Mackin ... Hello? Raymond Mackin here. Who is this?"

It was Dermot Glanville of the stock exchange.

"Raymond, I must speak to you!"

The man opposite sat forward and drank from his cup of coffee.

"Raymond, a director from a company called Transair International was arrested in Belfast last night. In his briefcase were a copies of R.M. & P. share contracts. The R.U.C. sent copies of the documents to the fraud squad in Dublin. We have been asked to investigate the matter. I am in my office at the moment. I think you had better come over to the exchange now!"

The line went dead. Mackin pocketed the phone.

"Excuse me. I could not help but overhear. You mentioned that your name was Raymond Mackin. Did your family live on Westminster Road in Foxrock by any chance?"

"Yes," Mackin answered, uninterested.

"My name is Dan Kinsella. I live in Cornelscourt. I used to deliver the post to your house. You were very young. You probably wouldn't remember."

"That's right," Mackin replied cynically.

"Whatever happened to your father?" Dan continued. "The last I heard was that he was living in Spain. He had a problem with his chest. ... Your mother, she was a fine woman! Is she still alive?"

"My father is dead. My mother now lives in America," Mackin answered.

Dan was desperate to talk. Mackin's mind was, for the moment, elsewhere.

"My son was in a car crash," Dan continued. "He is on a life support machine. The doctor doesn't seem too hopeful. He is in a coma at the moment. They are going to operate later on this morning."

"I see," Mackin said, finishing his coffee and standing up.

"Are you visiting somebody?" Dan enquired.

"My son James has a heart condition. He is on the priority transplant list," Mackin answered, folding his paper and leaving it on the table.

"It's ironic, isn't it?" Dan added. "Dr. Curry told me this morning that she thought that Shane was perhaps brain dead, but his heart was as strong as a horse's."

Mackin sat down again.

" ... and while it beats, there is always hope."

Dan swallowed hard. Mackin contemplated for a moment. He recollected what the nurse had said:

"Dr. Brennan told Dr. Curry that with those injuries he should be dead. Indeed, he said that if the truth be known Shane Kinsella would be better off dead."

Mackin lit a cigarette and left the restaurant. He walked to the washroom, freshened up, and took a taxi to the stock exchange in Anglesea Street.

Dermot Glanville was waiting for Mackin. He handed him a copy of the contract note the R.U.C. had sent to the fraud squad. Mackin recognised the contract instantly.

"Raymond, I have spoken to the president and the general manager of the exchange. Let it be said that, in the past, we have reluctantly supported your disputes with clients, even though some of them were dubious. In order to show a united front, we have allowed you the benefit of the doubt. This is, of course, another matter. I am not going to ask you how you got involved, but my information is that Transair International is a cover for a paramilitary organisation. Looking at the evidence, Raymond, it is clear that you laundered almost half a million pounds for your client. The president has demanded a full written report on his desk on Monday morning!"

Mackin stood and approached Glanville's desk. He picked up the contract, rolled it in a ball and tossed it towards a wicker basket in the corner. He walked out of the office, leaving the door open.

CHAPTER 9

Dan Kinsella picked up Mackin's discarded Irish Times and went back up to intensive care. Shane still lay on the bed motionless, every vital organ of his body connected to a vast array of life supporting medical equipment. Dan leaned on the bed and spoke to Shane.

"Come on, son. Wake up. You have your whole life ahead of you. If you can hear me, son, just move a finger, anything. Come on, son. You can do it. All your friends from school have sent you get-well cards. I will read you one ..."

Dan spoke to Shane for almost an hour. Exhausted, he finally sat down and unfolded the newspaper. There on the front page was a photograph of a crashed car and a report.

Last night in the quiet suburban village of Cabinteely in County Dublin, within yards of the local garda station, two young teenage joyriders knocked down and seriously injured a pedestrian waiting to cross the road. The man, in his late teens, had just purchased a magazine from the newsagents and was waiting to cross to the parish church. The stolen B.M.W. rounded a corner at high speed coming from the Bray direction. Witnesses watched in horror as the stolen car careered out of control, mounted the footpath, knocked down the young man and dragged him almost one hundred yards along the road before smashing into a traffic light. A hospital spokesman described the injured man's condition as critical.

Dan dropped the newspaper and sat up. He put his elbows on his knees, cradled his head in his hands and cried. Two nurses came to turn Shane.

"Are you all right, Mr. Kinsella? Would you like a cup of tea," one of the nurses enquired kindly.

"I'm sorry, nurse. No thank you. I just feel so helpless. So alone. If Shane dies, I don't know what I will do!"

At that moment, Dr. Curry appeared.

"Mr. Kinsella, I looked in on Shane earlier. I am afraid there has been no improvement. But, at the same time, he is stable. We will be carrying out the angiogram in a few moments, so I must ask you to wait outside. As I told you last night, we will know a little more this morning when the tests are complete. Your son's life is in the balance. We must, at all costs, make the correct diagnosis. That is why the angiogram is necessary."

Dan looked confused.

"Could you please explain what an angiogram is, doctor?"

"I am sorry, Mr. Kinsella. I thought I had explained last night. We must inject a radio-opaque substance into Shane's blood vessels in order to make them visible on x-ray. The operation is fairly routine, but of course it is not without its hazards!"

Dan left intensive care as the radiologist and the neuroradiologist arrived. Within minutes, Shane was prepared for the operation.

Dr. Curry inserted a needle and a thin rubber catheter or tube into Shane's femoral artery, then directed it from his groin up to the aortic arch and from there into the left carotid artery in his neck. A wire encased in the catheter enabled the doctor to guide it. Dr. Curry followed the catheter's progress on the image intensifier, which revealed the patient's entire arterial system. A nurse monitored his pulse. A falling pulse rate could signal a spasm, which in turn would have disastrous consequences.

Dr. Curry's eyes were fixed on the screen. This was the

critical moment: the injection of the dye which would allow the biplane x-ray cameras to simultaneously photograph his brain from the side and above. Not all patients can tolerate the dye. Dr. Curry proceeded cautiously. She injected a small amount of dye, then observed her patient and not the screen. Good. No hives, blotches or allergic reactions. She instructed the neuroradiologist to inject the entire dosage. The radiologist set both cameras. The photographs were taken and the films were removed and sent to the lab. The developed plates would reveal the full extent of the internal damage to Shane's brain without the need for complicated and dangerous surgery.

Dan sat all morning in the waiting room. He recalled the day Shane had arrived from the adoption agency, the excitement. Deirdre ran around the house, cleaning and dusting, checking her hair in the hall mirror, looking out across the green every couple of minutes, anxiously watching and waiting for the social worker's car to pull up. Deirdre's excitement was infectious. When the old Morris Minor finally arrived, every woman in the estate came running to see the new addition to the Kinsella family. Dan remembered Shane's smiling face and his sore ribs after the hours spent on all fours with Shane on his back kicking and shouting, "Giddy up horsey".

Dan was not prepared for the absolute strength of the love he had for Shane. He often wondered was he the son of a young, unmarried girl cast out by her family or perhaps the unwanted child of a wealthy businessman. Both he and Deirdre were besotted. Every night they would stand over Shane's cot, their arms intertwined, thanking God for their good fortune. Now Deirdre was dead and Shane was critically ill.

"Mr. Kinsella! ... Mr. Kinsella!"

Dr. Curry stood just inside the glass-panelled door of

the waiting room.

"I would like to speak to you, please … in my office."

Dr. Curry's office was neatly furnished, if spartan. The colour scheme was relaxing. Dan sat. He knew by Dr. Curry's face that the prognosis was not hopeful.

"Mr. Kinsella, I'm afraid that the x-rays from the angiogram confirmed our fears."

Dr. Curry placed an x-ray in the viewing box and continued solemnly.

"Shane has suffered a massive depressed fracture with associated left frontal lobe contusions, or bruises."

Dan looked drawn and confused. Dr. Curry continued.

"We are convinced that Shane has suffered irreversible brain damage and should he recover consciousness, which we feel is unlikely, he will almost certainly be severely mentally and physically handicapped."

Dan stood and walked over to the window overlooking the rear entrance to the hospital. An ambulance appeared, its siren echoing through the narrow laneway.

"At the moment," Dr. Curry continued, "Shane is in surgery. His respiratory pattern is irregular and there is pressure on his brain stem which must be relieved immediately. This pressure is of a grave concern and is caused by a haematoma, an accumulation of blood that leaks into the tissues. The surgeon will also remove any fragments of dead bone and non-viable brain tissue. Then all we can do is observe and monitor. I'm sorry if I appear brutal, but there is no benefit in giving you false hope."

CHAPTER 10

It was almost nine p.m. when Joan left the hospital. With dismay, she considered the two young men who remained behind. Mr. Kinsella may have felt that she had been unnecessarily graphic with him, but the truth was that she had sheltered him from the true horror of what was necessary to relieve the pressure from Shane's brain and prepared him from what she considered to be the inevitable conclusion.

James's demise was slow and equally heart-rending. Joan was helpless. The report she wrote stated:

James Mackin's condition continues to deteriorate. All we can do is make him as comfortable as possible and hope that a donor heart becomes available soon.

She considered Mackin. Despite everything, she could not allow her personal problems to interfere with her professional responsibilities. She consoled herself, believing that the stock exchange regulatory body would redress the balance.

The traffic along Sandymount and the Rock Road was slow. There had been a Rugby International in Lansdowne Road earlier. Now hundreds of inebriated Welsh rugby supporters were disrupting the traffic. Joan recalled a recent newspaper article.

Soccer supporters are described as hooligans. Similar behaviour from their counterparts, rugby supporters, is considered merely high spirited.

Joan locked her car and crossed the car park to the

canopied entrance porch of her apartment block. The air on the top of Killiney Hill was as always invigorating. She selected a brass key, opened the mahogany door and stepped into the tiled lobby. Unlike the rest of the luxurious apartment block, this area was cold and uninviting. She toyed with the idea of walking up the four flights of stairs to the apartment, but decided to take the lift. No matter how many times she used the lift, she always wondered how she would react if the lift got stuck between floors or what would happen if the cables snapped and the lift crashed into the basement.

A gush of warm air greeted Joan as she opened her front door. She stepped into the hallway of the apartment, hung up her coat and kicked off her shoes. The central heating boiler clicked on. Joan remembered that she hadn't rung the gas board. She picked up the phone in the sitting room and dialled the emergency number.

"Hello, this is Dr. Joan Curry. I am a little worried about my central heating boiler. I don't have much experience of gas heating and I have just moved into the apartment. I am just a little nervous. The time switch on the boiler is set but the heating does not always come on. I live alone and am out during the day, so I am terrified that I may blow up the whole apartment block."

"Don't worry, Dr. Curry. We will send somebody out to service your boiler tomorrow. Do you have a number we can contact you at during the day?"

Joan put the phone down and stood a moment in the dark. The moon shone into the sitting room. She walked to the window that ran the whole length of the penthouse and stared out at Dun Laoghaire Pier in the distance. The ferry had just arrived from Holyhead. Joan watched as hundreds of cars spilled out of the belly of the ship, passed through the customs hall and out onto Queen's Road.

Joan thought she heard a noise in the study. Must have left the television on, she reasoned. She began to unbutton her white surgical coat as she walked through the dining room and approached the study. She opened the study door. The light was off and the television was on. She knelt down and turned it off.

"I was watching that!" came a man's voice from behind.

Joan jumped to her feet and swung around. Her heart almost exploded.

"You were right to ring the gas board. You can never be too careful, can you? A woman alone. Make sure you see the engineer's identity card before you let him in."

"Who's there?" Joan screamed as she tried to run out the door. In the dark, the shape of a man moved to the doorway and blocked her exit. The man pushed her roughly to the floor.

"If you don't want to get hurt, you had better sit down and stay quiet! I have something I want to say and I am not leaving until I say it."

Joan thought she recognised the man's voice.

"Put on the lights!" she demanded.

"Are you going to behave yourself?" her attacker enquired.

Joan now knew who the intruder was. Raymond Mackin switched on the ceiling light. Joan was less afraid.

"What the hell are you doing in my apartment? I'm going to call the police."

"I don't think so, doctor."

Mackin walked over to the telephone, ripped the wires out of the wall, then flung the instrument on the floor. His eyes were wild. A vein palpitated in his neck. The man terrified Joan. He returned to the door and stared long and hard at her. He then removed a bunch of keys from his jacket pocket, selected two and placed them on the coffee table. He now spoke calmly.

"I found these spare keys to the apartment in my car. I was in the locality and thought that I should drop them in. While I'm here, there is something else I would like to talk to you about!"

Mackin noticed that something had fallen out of Joan's white surgical coat onto the carpet. He leaned down and picked it up.

"What do you mean spare keys?" Joan enquired. "How would you have spare keys to my apartment?"

"Simple," Mackin explained. "This was my apartment. I sold it to you. Your cousin Eileen's death was indeed most fortuitous … for me!"

Mackin was at his ease. He was now totally in control. Joan, however, was trying to come to terms with the fact that in the past weeks Mackin had turned her financial security into a disaster. Joan had purchased the apartment on the basis of the funds due to her from the sale of the Skellig shares. Mackin had sold them as instructed, but had re-invested the money in Fastnet shares, which had subsequently halved in value.

Crouched on the floor, leaning back against a chair, Joan considered the fact that she was, as a consequence of Mackin's dealings, living in an apartment she could no longer afford. The bridging loan from the bank, secured on the pending sale of the shares, would be withdrawn and the apartment subsequently sold to pay her debts.

"I called," Mackin continued, "to collect the money you owe me."

"I have written to the stock exchange!" Joan retorted, hoping that the threat would gain her an advantage. It had the opposite effect. Mackin laughed loudly and madly.

"The stock exchange. Oh, heavens! I'm in big trouble

now!" Mackin mocked. "You stupid woman!"

The fire returned to Mackin's eyes. He moved across to where Joan sat and stood menacingly over her. Joan remained tense and offered no resistance.

"The stock exchange ... the stock exchange is as corrupt as the people it harbours. It is run by a band of men grown accustomed to the easy life. They will do nothing, absolutely nothing. Do you really expect them to regulate against their friends and colleagues? I want my money and I want it now! Maybe, of course, you would prefer to deal with some other, less understanding associates of mine."

Mackin returned to the door and removed what looked like a small business card from the breast pocket of his jacket. He smiled broadly as he spoke.

"Today I met a man who used to deliver the post to my father's house. He told me about his son, who had been knocked down by a car and was now in a coma. Before that, I overheard a nurse say that Dr. Brennan had told you that with those injuries this man's son should be dead. Indeed, he said that in his opinion the boy would be better off dead."

"What has all this got to do with you?" Joan demanded.

"You're not as clever as you think, doctor. It's quite simple!"

Mackin placed the card on the table. Joan picked it up. She recognised it instantly. It was Shane Kinsella's organ donor card. It must have been in her pocket since she picked it up in the ambulance.

"This young man is as good as dead. According to his father, you told him that even though his brain is dead his heart is still strong."

"I still have no idea what you are getting at!" Joan interrupted.

"It's simple! Kinsella's son doesn't need his heart. My

son does. Switch off Kinsella's life support machine and transplant his heart into James. Now do you understand?"

Joan was no longer confused. Mackin was suggesting that she terminate Shane's life and transplant his healthy heart to his son James.

"Mr. Mackin, I am asking you to leave my home this instant. What you are suggesting is preposterous and not worthy of any consideration at all."

To her surprise, Mackin began to withdraw. He walked back through the dining room and lounge. Joan followed tentatively. At the front door he turned to face Joan.

"Dr. Curry, you have come across a relentless force. You have not heard the last of this. Bear in mind that the solution is simple. If you switch off the machine, I will clear your debt. If not, I will buy back your apartment from the receivers at my price!"

CHAPTER 11

On Monday morning, Mackin turned into the car park in front of his office. It was eight o'clock. Noreen's car was parked outside. He drove on to the hospital. His car phone rang.

"Raymond Mackin?"

"You were looking for me," came the man's voice on the other end of the phone.

"Yes, I have a job for you. Meet me behind the Mater Hospital in Leo Street at one o'clock." Mackin replaced the phone in its cradle.

As he entered James's private room, Mackin saw that Veronica was seated on James's bed talking to Dr. Curry. Both women ignored him and continued with their conversation. James lay back and pressed his cheek against Veronica's hand. Dr. Curry noted that James became inhibited in his father's presence. Mackin's hostility engulfed the room and reflected his rigid state of mind. James, aside from drowsiness due to medication, seemed healthy, if withdrawn. He stared at his father suspiciously. He was frightened. Mackin's parental deprivation had inflicted a lifelong emotional sentence on James.

Dr. Curry left the room. James closed his eyes and slept peacefully.

"We need to talk!" Veronica ordered.

"What about?" Mackin sighed.

"Wait for me outside!" Veronica pointed to the door.

Mackin stood in the hall while Veronica fixed James's bed.

"You are in trouble. Dr. Curry suspects that James has been the victim of mental and physical abuse."

"I never laid a finger on James. I defy any man or

woman to prove that I did!" Mackin was incensed. Veronica slapped him hard across the face.

"Raymond," Veronica screamed, "your problem is that you consider everyone except yourself to be a fool. Believe me, these people are highly skilled professionals and, unlike me, are not gullible. Every day they deal with cases concerning the mind and body. They took x-rays. Not even you can explain away the fractures. This is the worst week of my life and I have you to support me? You have never loved me or James. I was an accessory, James a disappointment. You know the funny thing about all this is that your first child, the one you forced me to put up for adoption, appears to be everything you ever wanted. But your selfishness condemned him to obscurity. Well, despite you, he has grown and developed into a strong, normal eighteen-year-old who starts in medical school next term.

"What are you talking about? How do you know all this."

"It was so easy for you to have him adopted. But I was his mother. I had to drive to the convent and hand over the child I carried for nine months to an anonymous nun and then spend the next eighteen years wondering whatever happened to him. Well, he wrote and wants to meet me and I wrote back. But believe me, Raymond Mackin, for as long as I live you will never get the opportunity to break this child's spirit like you broke James's. One thing you can be sure of is, when this is all over, I want a separation. Believe me, the girl you married is now a woman and I will take you for everything you have."

In shock, Mackin took the lift down to the ground floor. At reception he followed the sign for intensive care. Cautiously, he opened the door and entered the intensive care unit. The nurses were changing shifts. Mackin, in his dark suit, had the appearance of a consultant.

"Can I help you doctor?" a pretty nurse enquired.

"Yes, nurse. I am looking for mmm … Kinsella."

Mackin could not think of young Kinsella's Christian name. Stupid really, he thought, as it was the same name Veronica chose for the child they had put up for adoption. The nurse led Mackin over to Shane Kinsella's bed.

"Thank you, nurse."

Mackin looked at the boy lying in the bed. His head was covered in bandages. He was lifeless. Two nurses came over to the bed.

"Excuse me, doctor. We just have to turn the patient."

As they moved Shane to avoid pressure sores, the bandage dropped to expose his hideously deformed and shaven head. There were stitches all around the top of his head. Mackin turned away. It was as if the doctors had taken the top of his skull off to probe inside. On the side of his head there were holes which had been bored into Shane's skull to drain fluids from his ravaged brain.

"It's not looking too good for Shane, doctor, is it?" one of the nurses spoke directly to Mackin.

"No!" Mackin replied.

Even though Shane was connected up to a variety of monitors and support machines, the nurse still checked his blood pressure, respiration rate, temperature and pulse and recorded her findings on the observation chart.

Mackin regarded the bank of life saving machinery and followed the wires along the wall to three power points into which all the machinery was plugged. How simple it would be, he thought as he left intensive care.

CHAPTER 12

D an was now an unhappy, solemn fixture in the restaurant. The nurses continually offered words of encouragement. Dan enjoyed the attention. He was by nature a solitary man, but here in the hospital he had celebrity status. Back in Cornelscourt he had few friends. When he was younger, he dedicated his time to playing semi-professional football with Drumcondra. When he married, he chose to dedicate his time to providing for his family. His parents were dead almost ten years now. Both died within weeks of each other. His mother, the doctor had said, died of a broken heart. His brother lived in Knutsford, a small village just outside Manchester, near the airport. He owned a garage and dealt in classic and veteran cars. They were close once, but had drifted apart.

Dan drank a cup of tea while he idly thumbed through a magazine. At that moment any sound, any word, good or bad, would have been welcome. He looked at his watch. It was almost mid-day. Dr. Curry would be doing her rounds. As he entered intensive care, Dan passed a young girl being rushed in on a stretcher. She had been knocked off her bicycle. "No helmet!" he heard the ambulance man say. The child was in shock. Her mother was on the phone, frantically looking for her husband. A nurse stood beside the woman, trying to console her.

Dr. Curry was examining Shane. Dan wandered over to the window and waited for her to complete her examination. There was no improvement. He wasn't blind. He could see that. Dan stared at the back of the buildings on Dorset Street, then down at the laneway below. His eyes focused on a car parked behind the hospital. He clearly observed Raymond Mackin sitting in his Mercedes. He was speaking on his mobile phone. Moments later, an old blue Ford Transit van pulled up beside him. Two men got out of the van and went over to Mackin's car. One was young, tall and athletic, the other middle-aged, bearded, small and squat. They spoke for a few moments and nodded their heads. Mackin handed the older man an envelope. He examined the contents before both men climbed back into the van and drove off.

"Mr. Kinsella?"

"Sorry ... How is he doctor?"

"To be honest, Mr. Kinsella, even you can see Shane's condition is deteriorating. His brain stem, we believe, has ceased to function. If we withdraw the ventilator at this juncture, his heart will stop beating within minutes. In short, our opinion is that Shane is brain dead."

"How do you know he is brain dead?" Dan pleaded. Deep in his subconscious, he had already accepted Shane's death, but the finality of what Dr. Curry was saying suddenly struck him.

"Mr. Kinsella, at the moment we can't be positive, but there have been careful guidelines laid down for diagnosing brain death. We have the evidence of the angiogram, the C.T. scan, indicating large areas of dead brain tissue, and the surgeon's subsequent findings during surgery. Shane still does not respond to painful stimuli, his pupils are fixed and all normal reflexes are absent. There is, however, one other test that we must carry out before we can say for definite that Shane is brain dead. These tests are conducted by two independent clinicians and are repeated after twenty-four hours. Mr. Kinsella, my job is to prolong life, not to take it away unnecessarily. Shane has suffered a massive trauma and, if these final tests confirm that the brain stem has been irreversibly damaged, then the kindest thing for Shane would be to withdraw artificial ventilation and allow Shane to die with dignity."

"What you mean, doctor, is to switch off the life support machine?"

"Yes," Dr. Curry replied solemnly.

"How long will he live then?" Dan enquired.

"That depends. As I said, his heart is strong."

"I suppose, then, there is nothing else to do but wait?"

"Actually, there is."

Dr. Curry took a deep breath and removed Shane's organ donor card from her pocket. She handed it to Dan. His hands were shaking as he grasped the card.

"Mr. Kinsella, it was Shane's wish that when he died his organs would go to benefit others. It is through the generosity of organ donors like Shane and their families that so many lives have been saved and such huge strides have been made in modern medicine."

CHAPTER 13

Before Dr. Curry left the hospital, she called to see James. Veronica had gone home. She was not expected back for at least an hour. This was the first time she had been able to speak to James alone. Some of his school friends had been in earlier and he was tired. He lay on his side, idly playing a miniature computer game. Apart from his somewhat gaunt appearance, it was hard to believe that this cheerful youth was battling a life-threatening illness. James looked up, saw Dr. Curry standing at the end of his bed and put the game down.

"Dr. Curry can I ask you a question and will you promise to tell me the truth?"

"If I can."

"Am I going to die?"

Dr. Curry was startled by the directness of the question.

"James, we are all going to die. There is no denying you are very ill. Your heart is failing and, as a consequence, you have been put on the priority list for a heart transplant."

"The operation ... how dangerous is it?"

"The procedure itself is reasonably straightforward. Bear in mind that the first successful heart transplant was performed over twenty-five years ago and the technique has changed very little since. What has changed is the anti-rejection drugs. The after-care of the patient is of primary importance. What we have to guard against is rejection and infection. First though, James, we must find you a strong donor heart!"

"What are my chances, doctor, if you find a donor heart?"

"Rejection of the new organ is, as I said, a major problem. It is true to say that many of the first patients to undergo heart transplant surgery died. Their bodies literally waged war on the new organs. With kidneys, they found that members of the same family, especially twins, were more likely to be genetically matched, so their likelihood of survival was greater. In your case, fortunately, you and your family each have two working kidneys, but only one heart."

James laughed nervously.

"Originally patients were given steroids, but they did more harm than good. But since the late sixties, immuno-suppressive drugs were successfully developed and refined. What they do is suppress the body's natural instinct to attack the new organ and their success has led to today's excellent survival rate."

James had drifted to sleep. Dr. Curry checked his chart and left.

As she walked past the nurses' station, Dr. Curry saw Veronica Mackin. She was seated alone in the television room. She was staring blankly at the wall. Dr. Curry opened the door and walked in. Veronica turned to face her. She smiled. In her left hand she held a letter, in her right a single red rose. She had been crying. She folded up the letter and placed it in her handbag.

"I was just in with James," Dr. Curry explained. "You look distressed. Would you like to talk, Mrs. Mackin."

Veronica Mackin looked at the doctor suspiciously.

"It's not fair of me to burden you with my problems, doctor!"

"For as long as James is a patient in this hospital, his welfare is my responsibility and, as a consequence, your problems are mine!"

Veronica relaxed back into her chair.

"When I was eighteen, I met and fell in love with my husband. I became pregnant. Raymond and his family

80

wanted me to have an abortion. My family, however, sent me to stay with my aunt. She lived on a farm close to Macroom. When the baby was born, it was to be offered up for adoption. I had the child, a little boy. He was a beautiful baby and I was besotted. I sat all day watching and holding him. I was not prepared for the overwhelming feeling of love that I had for him. It upset me that such an innocent child was cast out by society and that his father had chosen to totally ignore his existence. On the day he was to handed up to the nuns, I just lay on the floor of the farmhouse, playing and talking to him. I told him how much I loved him and hoped that one day he might understand why I had to give him up. I cut off a piece of his hair and had it mounted in a locket. Raymond found it when I returned to Dublin. He tossed it in the fire.

"'This is your past Veronica,' he told me. 'You must look to the future!'

"I hate Raymond Mackin, doctor. He is evil and capable of anything. Don't ever cross him."

Veronica nervously lit a cigarette and continued.

"I was distraught and rang the convent. They told me that the child had to be brought in before eight o'clock that night. I dressed him warmly and took him for a walk. I carried him for hours through the fields and woods, talking to him. When it became dark, we returned to the farmhouse. I bathed, powdered and dressed him in his best clothes. My uncle drove us to the convent. We sat outside in the car until one minute to eight. A nun greeted me at the hall door and led me down a long corridor to the registrar's office. I knew at that moment that I would never see my baby again."

Veronica's eyes filled with tears. She fought with her memories.

"And the sound. That sound ... of my shoes clicking on

the tiles as I ran back down the corridor and out of the convent. I had signed my baby's life away."

Veronica stopped talking and turned her head away. The tears were now cascading down her cheeks. She was a woman tormented by her past. She was inconsolable.

There was a knock on the door. It was Raymond Mackin. Veronica sat up, dried her eyes, thanked Dr. Curry for listening and walked over to her husband standing in the doorway.

"What are you crying for?" he asked impatiently as she passed him and walked down the corridor.

"You will never know!" she hissed.

୫ ୫ ୫

It was almost eight p.m. when Joan finally arrived home. She collected her post. There were a lot of letters. One in particular, she noted, looked official. She opened and read it upstairs in the kitchen as she drank a cup of tea. It was a solicitor's letter.

Dear Madame,

We act on behalf of R.M. & P. Stockbrokers Limited and have been instructed to write to you in relation to an outstanding debt of £11,000 in respect of the purchase by our client of Pacific shares on your behalf.

Enclosed is a copy statement of account. You are requested to discharge the amount outstanding within seven days from the date hereof. Failing hearing from you, our instructions are to issue proceedings without further notice and to seek interest and costs thereon. We await hearing from you and would be obliged if you would note that all further communications relating to this matter should be directed to this firm.

The phone rang. Joan got a fright.

"Hello."

"Could I speak to Dr. Joan Curry, please?" It was a man's voice.

"Dr. Curry, my name is Fred Hanley. I am a journalist with The Business Post. I am putting together a story on a Dublin stockbroker. It is an exposé. I am informed that you may have encountered some problems with this man. If so, you are not the first. But I would like to think that you may be one of the last when the story is printed."

Joan had not recovered from the shock of the solicitor's letter. She still held it in her hand.

"I was wondering, doctor, could I call to see you tonight? The article is being published next Sunday."

"Yes, of course," Joan answered. "Call after nine."

Joan put the phone down. She was incensed and utterly bewildered. How could everything go so wrong in such a short time. There were so many mixed emotions. She looked around the apartment and began to panic. She was still on bridging finance. There was a letter from the bank. She opened it, knowing the contents.

Dear Dr. Curry,

Re: Bridging Finance

With reference to the above facility extended to you by the bank. I must inform you that unless …

Joan put the letter down on the kitchen table.

CHAPTER 14

Noreen Harte peered through a small gap in the door of Raymond Mackin's office. The managing director of R.M. & P. was working late. He reclined in an executive chair with his back to her, reading a report. Noreen edged forward into the office. She wondered for a moment what inner modem drove a man like Raymond Mackin. The man had built his business on the misfortunes of his clients. He was completely devoid of compassion or feeling towards those he crushed. He was an evil man, so wrapped up in self-gratification that he could not appreciate that he was pushing people beyond the threshold of their endurance.

"I remember," he told Noreen one day, "as a child reading a story about a lowly accounts clerk in the welfare department in New York. This fifty-year-old spinster took one cent from each welfare cheque of the forty thousand she ran weekly. Nobody noticed or bothered to complain as she diverted four thousand dollars into her own bank account each week." Noreen now wondered was Mackin making the same mistake. The accounts clerk worked the fraud for over two years, then became greedy and was ultimately discovered.

Noreen was aware that if an investigation was carried out by the stock exchange into R.M. & P., she would certainly be implicated in many of Mackin's fraudulent dealings. After much deliberation, she confided in Bernard Hannigan. They decided to approach the stock exchange regulatory body and report Mackin. They demanded confidentiality and explained to the officer that they were inexperienced and did not fully understand the consequences of what they were doing. The stock exchange were less than helpful and claimed that there was insufficient evidence. Bernard Hannigan had a friend who was a journalist in The Business Post. In anger and desperation, they decided to speak to him.

Mackin's phone rang. He swung around and noticed Noreen standing in the doorway. He gestured for her to enter and answered the phone. The call came through on his private line.

"Raymond, I thought I'd better give you a call."

"Who is this?" Mackin demanded.

"Richard fromThe Business Post ."

"Go on, what is it?"

"Something that will be of interest to you has just this minute come across my desk. They are running a feature this Sunday about R.M. & P... It's an exposé. I have seen the rough draft and it's not very complimentary. A freelance journalist called Fred Hanley has been doing the investigations."

"They would not dare!" Mackin roared. "If they print the story, I will transfer all future advertising features toThe Tribune. If the editor thinks that he can afford to lose a fifty thousand pound account, which is a lot of newspapers, then let him print the damn story. Tell him that if he prints one word out of place, I will string him up. Do I make myself clear?"

"There is something else you should know," Richard continued. "Hanley's talking with two of your employees."

"Who?" demanded Mackin.

"According to his notes, a girl called Noreen Harte and a Bernard Hannigan."

Mackin thought for a moment then laughed.

"The story holds no credence. Both of them were sacked earlier this week for running their own book. It's only ... a woman scorned!"

Mackin replaced the phone and regarded Noreen intensely.

"Sit down!"

Mackin picked up the phone and dialled an internal phone number.

"Bernard. Ah, you're still here. Would you mind dropping up to my office for a moment?"

Mackin stood and walked around the office. Noreen followed his movements. She was drained of all emotion. Hannigan appeared at the door.

"Come in, Bernard. Sit down."

Mackin closed the door behind Hannigan as he sat down.

"I have evidence that both of you have been running your own book within the company, disadvantaging my clients. Hannigan, last Friday you created a market to sell Pacific shares that were in your own account."

"That's not true. You told me to buy those shares and put them in your account. They were your shares!" Hannigan defended.

"You know that I know that, but when they come to investigate they will find the shares in your account and I will give them a tape of you instructing the dealer to create the market. Noreen, I believe you countersigned the deals."

The stark reality of the situation struck Noreen. A few simple alterations on the computer and Mackin could intimate that the fraudulent deal was carried out by herself and Bernard Hannigan.

"I want both of you," Mackin continued, "to clear your desks and vacate your offices immediately ... and Noreen, don't forget to drop me in the keys of the car and the apartment."

CHAPTER 15

Dan sat at the end of Shane's bed. He had been joined by Father O'Connell, who had wrapped his rosary beads around Shane's limp, lifeless hands. The nurses came and turned him again. He had lost so much weight in so little time.

Dan wished that he had faith. He remembered, as a young boy in the convent, carrying his Bible with him everywhere, how he donated his pocket money to the African missions and every spare penny to the black babies. He had learned all the prayers in his catechism. Every Friday, he would eat fish and go to confession. On Sunday, he would go to mass and receive Holy Communion. During his summer holidays, he would go to mass every morning. He was terrified that he might touch the host with his teeth. When he was old enough, he served mass. He remembered the day he sneaked a look at the priest raising the chalice when the bell rang during the offertory. He waited for a bolt of lightning to blast him to hell. Then, as he got older, he went to secondary school and encountered the Christian Brothers, who were anything but Christian. The parochial house was divided into two. The two priests living there had their own kitchen, bedroom, sitting room, housekeeper and letterbox. He wondered how these men could preach charity, humility and kindness to their parishioners yet they could not live together themselves.

Dan remembered vividly the day his father died and how the family had gathered around. He admired the strength that his aunt appeared to cull from her religious beliefs. He too wanted to believe that one day he would be reunited with his father. He choked back the tears as he recalled the day his father was told by the doctor that he was dying.

"Mr. Kinsella, your lung cancer is terminal. There are secondaries. We will carry out radiation and chemotherapy. However, I must inform you that we are not too hopeful that this treatment will be beneficial. We are really looking for miracles. I suggest that you take this opportunity to ensure that your affairs are in order."

His father had asked for the truth, but did not expect such frankness delivered without a lifeline. Within twenty minutes, his father had effectively given up the fight. He may have had only weeks to live, but this doctor had in a selfish, unguarded moment obliterated what lucid time that may have remained. Dan remembered the long hours sitting by his father's bed, stroking his head and wiping the sweat from his brow after his body had been ravaged by the drugs that were supposed to cure him. Watching a strong muscular man with a fierce pride disintegrate with each forced breath was harrowing. It was as if he were drowning in his own phlegm. All the images flashed by: the day a junior doctor spent twenty minutes trying to find a vein to administer morphine that no longer appeared to ease the pain, the subsequent increase in dosage that eventually rendered his father senseless. There were the awful moments when his father's body stiffened as it was raked in agony and the mournful look that followed the grimace. Dan remembered the kisses. His father's cold stubbled face that had once smelled of old spice, now exhumed disinfectant. The nurses, those wonderful women who try to detach themselves, could be seen crying in quiet corners. He recalled the final moment when that last forced breath faded away and silence and dignity returned after death.

"I think, Dan, that the Lord has already taken Shane. All that remains is his soul. Perhaps it is time to release his spirit from this world and allow him to move to the next!"

Father O'Connell spoke quietly.

"I know that you have never been a religious man, but will you join me in a prayer for Shane."

Distressed as Dan was, he was grateful that Shane did not have to endure the same agony and humiliation as his father.

The two men knelt. Around them doctors, nurses and ambulance men ran to and fro. As he prayed, Dan observed a confused old woman who had wandered in from casualty. She complained to a doctor that one of the nurses was trying to murder her. The old man in the bed next to Shane's suddenly began to gasp for breath. A doctor and two nurses came running. The old man sat up, his eyes darting around the room. His head began to shake. Slowly at first, then violently. He fell back limp into the arms of a nurse. Dan turned away.

Two men dressed in overalls watched Father O'Connell and Dan as they prayed. One was in his late forties, squat, bald with a neatly trimmed dark beard. The younger man in his twenties was taller and more heavily built with a shaved head. They walked over and spoke to Dan.

"Your son?" the older man enquired.

"Yes," replied Dan.

CHAPTER 16

Joan sat alone in the dark, still clutching the crumpled letter from the bank.

The buzzer on the intercom sounded. Joan ignored it. ... It sounded again. This time, she got up slowly and placed the letter on the coffee table. She looked at the monitor. There were two men in the reception area standing before the security camera. She picked up the phone.

"Yes," Joan said impatiently.

"Is that Dr. Curry?" one of the men enquired.

"Yes."

"We are from the gas board. You reported a problem with your central heating boiler."

Joan had forgotten that the gas board were to call. She looked at her watch. It was twenty to nine. She told them she was on the fourth floor, then pressed the button and allowed them in. She waited by the front door, looking through the spy hole.

Two men came out of the lift. They were dressed in navy overalls. Joan noted that they carried no tools. One was a small bearded man in his forties. The other was a much younger man in his early twenties. He was over six foot and his head was shaved.

"Could you show us where the central heating boiler is, miss?"

Joan led them into the utility room where the gas burner was located. The two men followed.

The older man opened a door which led out onto the tiled balcony that surrounded the penthouse apartment.

"Best to keep the room ventilated." he explained.

"My name is Pat," the squat man with the beard informed Joan. "This is my son Colm."

Suddenly, Joan was grabbed from behind. An arm went around her throat and held her in a vice-like grip. She could not breathe. She raised her hands to ease the pressure on her throat, but her arms were pulled roughly behind her back and tied with rope. As she turned to face her attacker, a hood was placed over her head and the cord pulled tight.

"I would suggest, doctor, if you intend seeing any of your patients again, that you stop struggling and don't scream."

The hood was loosened and raised enough for Joan to see a long blade knife and the smiling face of the younger man. The cord was tightened again.

"Do I make myself understood?" he added.

Joan nodded, then stumbled forward, falling over the clothes basket. The men laughed. Joan sat in the dark, fighting for her breath.

"I can't breathe!" she cried.

"Well, doctor, maybe you would like some gas?" Pat offered, mocking Joan's accent.

Joan heard one of the men blow out the pilot light.

"We will be outside, doctor, if you want to speak to us. Be careful of the step. It would be a shame if you fell off the balcony."

"Talk about what?" Joan pleaded.

"Just talk ... right?" Colm demanded.

Joan sat on the floor, her head spinning. She dared not move. She became faint and struggled in vain to get to her feet. Her initial reaction was one of curiosity more than concern. Her analytical brain groped for a logical explanation for what was happening. Her eyes were on fire and her lungs felt as if they were going to explode from the gas fumes.

"Want some fresh air, doctor?"

Joan recognised Pat's voice. He dragged Joan out onto

the balcony. It was cold and the wind was rising. He walked Joan around to the front of the building.

"Are you ready to talk now?"

"Yes, of course I am! But I don't for the life of me understand about what." Joan was becoming anxious. "If it's money you are looking for, there is over fifty pounds in my handbag and my banklink card is in my purse."

"Quiet, doctor. You are making too much noise!" The squat man with the beard was becoming angry.

"What do you want from me?" Joan shouted. Her voice was drowned out by the traffic. The younger man struck Joan across the back of the head.

"We said to keep quiet!"

Before the words had left his lips, Joan was lifted from behind and placed upon the balcony wall overlooking the car park four floors below. The older man removed Joan's hood.

"I would hate you to miss the view," he said.

"Now, I want you to listen to what I have to say. It is very straightforward. All you have to do is say one simple word: Yes!"

Pat placed the point of the knife in Joan's ear. He twisted it around slowly. Joan could feel the warm trickle of blood in her ear. She looked down at the car park four floors below.

"Just please tell me what you want from me," Joan tried to be calm.

"A friend of ours has a sick son."

"I will see him any time you want," Joan interrupted. "If that is all, it is ..."

The young man grabbed Joan's hair and pushed her head forward. Joan instinctively leaned back. She was terrified.

"I will not tell you again. Another word and we will see

if you can fly. The gardai will think you just couldn't take the pressure."

The young man twisted his fingers tightly around Joan's hair.

"Mr. Mackin's son is already a patient of yours. We are informed that he has only days to live. Unless, that is, he receives a donor heart."

"You don't understand. I cannot manufacture or produce a spare heart. Believe me, at times I wish I could."

"That, Dr. Curry, is where you are wrong. We can help. We have found you a spare heart. You have another patient: Shane Kinsella. We were in earlier to see him. He's as good as dead according to his father. Now you have a choice ... either you switch off Shane's life support machine or we do. We think it would be better if you did it. The boy dies with dignity, you transplant his heart to Mr. Mackin's son and he will show his gratitude by cancelling your debt. What could be fairer or simpler than that?"

"It's not as easy as that!" Joan pleaded.

"Doctor, you have twenty-four hours!"

The men pulled Joan down off the wall and led her inside. The young man turned on the lights in the apartment. He found the letter from the bank on the coffee table.

"And the bank manager's happy too!"

The buzzer on the intercom sounded. Joan looked at the men.

"Who is it?" the older man asked.

Joan looked at her watch. It was nine p.m.. At first, she could not think of who it might be. Then she remembered. It must be Fred Hanley, the journalist who called earlier.

"It's a colleague of mine. He said he might call."

"Don't answer it!" the younger man instructed.

The buzzer sounded again. The man downstairs fidgeted angrily in the entrance porch.

"Dr. Curry. It's Fred Hanley of The Business Post. Could you let me in please?"

"I thought you said he was a friend of yours? You lied to me."

The younger man grabbed Joan and threw her against the wall. Joan fell, limp as a puppet, into the marble fireplace, cracking her head on the brass surround as she fell. The older man tried to restrain him.

"Don't be stupid, Colm. She's no good to us dead."

The buzzer sounded yet again.

"Dr. Curry, it's the gas board. You called the emergency hotline last night."

Colm and Pat looked at each other and calmly walked to the front door.

"Not a word, doctor, or we will be back!"

CHAPTER 17

Raymond Mackin watched from his window as Noreen and Bernard Hannigan left the office. Noreen looked up and smiled. Mackin stood back. He returned to his desk and read a fax copy of Dr. Curry's letter of complaint to the stock exchange. He laughed, gathered up his papers and left the building.

In the car park, he placed his briefcase in the boot. To his annoyance, he noticed that one of his tyres was flat. He cursed. Fortunately, there was a taxi outside the gate. He sat in and asked the driver to take him to the Mater Hospital.

"Certainly, sir."

Before Mackin had time to react, the door of the taxi opened and a tall muscular man eased into the seat beside him.

"This taxi is taken," Mackin said to the man.

"Yes, I know," the man replied. "Take us to headquarters, Jack."

The man looked long and hard at Mackin.

"You have been instructed to attend a meeting."

When the car stopped at the traffic lights at Leeson Street Bridge, Mackin sat forward, concealing the fact that he was trying to open the door.

"You are wasting your time, pal! Save your energy. The door doesn't open. It's welded closed." The men laughed.

For the first time in his life, Raymond Mackin was in a situation he could not control. It unnerved him. A great anger and fear welled up inside him. Common sense, however, prevailed.

As they entered Camden Street, Mackin was told to lie face down on the floor of the car. He obeyed. The car continued on for another five minutes. Stopping outside a row of double-fronted red brick cottages. Mackin was bundled out of the car and into the house. He could hear men's voices as he was led into a room heated only by a single bar electric fire. The room was lit by a row of candles stretched across a cast iron fireplace. Seven men observed Mackin from the shadows. A man in a brown duffel coat came forward.

"Word is that you have been greedy, Mr. Mackin. We offered you a lucrative business. All we asked for in return was discretion and integrity. You have already failed us on one count and the council is not pleased. I have been asked to ensure that you understand where we are coming from and where you could end up. Your life has no value. From what I hear, if you were found floating in the Liffey, the gardai would have an extensive list of suspects, all with reasonable motives. We don't need any such reasons."

Mackin remained silent throughout.

"Consider this as your first and only warning."

An hour later Mackin, badly shaken, was left at the Mater Hospital.

He sat alone with James. They had little in common. It was almost midnight. The hospital was quiet. They watched television. An old Steve McQueen film *The Hunter* was on the movie channel. It was about a bounty hunter who spent his time chasing fugitives who had jumped bail. The chase eventually turns full circle and the hunter becomes the quarry of a vengeful psychopath. Mackin thought at the time it was ironic.

James was not interested. He watched his father. He hated his father, but also wanted to please him. He was lucid now and felt quite strong. He found it difficult to believe that his life hung by a thread. He recalled his sheltered childhood and how every morning his father dropped him to school and his mother collected him in the evening. James found it embarrassing. It was a private secondary school set in large gardens on Clyde Road. There were only one hundred and twenty students in the school. It was more like an extended family. James was an oddity in the school. He was not allowed to play any contact sports in case he was hurt. He so much wanted to fence, box and play rugby with the other boys. He even had to stay in the classroom during the morning and lunch breaks while the other boys played football, in the yard in winter and on the lawn in summer.

He remembered his first heart attack. He was twelve. He had felt particularly unwell that morning, a strange bloated feeling. He said nothing to his father on the way to school. There was a flu virus at the time so he was not unduly worried. It happened during physics class. The teacher was carrying out an experiment with mercury. James felt tired at first, then he experienced a wave of hot flushes followed by pains across his shoulders. Without warning, he began to vomit violently. His vision became distorted and almost dreamlike. Everything appeared in black and white. The next thing he remembered was lying on the floor of the classroom, then being wheeled into the intensive care department of St. Vincent's Hospital. He knew he was sick when the young nurse ran out of the room screaming for a doctor.

James despised everything about his father, particularly the way he treated his mother. At an early age, he had learned to accept that he was a grave disappointment to his father, but the mental cruelty that his father inflicted upon his mother through detachment and disinterest left James fraught with anger and hate. Over the years, his father had reduced her self-esteem to such a low level that she lost all confidence in herself and abandoned all her friends.

James was unsure of what to expect from the heart transplant. Dr. Curry had explained that even if a donor heart became available there was no guarantee that it would be suitable. Over the years, he had grown accustomed to this shortness of breath and tiredness, but he realised that day by day his breathing was becoming more laboured.

A couple of months earlier, he had watched a documentary about a group of people who were in urgent need of various transplants. James could not forget this particular young businessman who, like himself, required a heart transplant. The man was interviewed at home one night sitting in his living room before a log fire. He was twenty-nine years old, married with two young children. His young daughter crawled over the back of the patterned easy chair he sat on. She rolled down on top of him. He hugged and kissed her. His pretty blonde wife, ravaged by a host of conflicting emotions, was destitute. She did not reflect her husband's optimism. Parked in the gravel driveway of his country estate in Berkshire was a red Jaguar XJS. The night of the documentary, he had been put on stand-by. A donor heart had become available. The specialist was checking its suitability. The man was alert, witty and looking forward with confidence to his transplant. When the credits rolled at the end of the program, however, it said that an hour after the interview Jeremy was called into the hospital. Unfortunately, the following day his body rejected the donor heart and he died.

CHAPTER 18

A t six thirty a.m., Dan Kinsella sat on the steps outside the casualty department of the Mater Hospital. A group of teenagers who had been involved in a minor car accident earlier set off for home. They were minus one of their friends. A young girl was kept in for observation. Hopefully, they had learned a cheap lesson. One of the young men would have some explaining to do, however. His mother's Mitsubishi Colt would not be in her driveway this morning as it was wrapped around a pole on the South Circular Road. He had waited until his parents had gone to bed before slipping the car keys from his mother's handbag, sneaking downstairs, rolling the car out of the gate and driving it into town.

Back inside the hospital, Dan found Fr. O'Connell. They went for a cup of coffee.

"How do you feel, Dan?" Fr. O'Connell enquired.

"I have been better, father. I just wish I had your faith, something to embrace when I am alone. I have come to terms with the fact that Shane has effectively left me. I just want some news to grapple with, either way. Whatever the doctor says will come as a relief! ... Am I wrong, father, to think like this?"

"No, Dan. The body has its own way of dealing with grief. There are no set guidelines. You have been a good father to Shane and now his father in heaven awaits him."

As they entered the intensive care unit, Dr. Curry was consulting with another doctor.

"Mr. Kinsella, that was Dr. Brennan. He carried out the second independent series of tests last night and I am afraid, as we expected, he has reached the same conclusions as myself. I am sorry, Mr. Kinsella ... Shane is, without doubt, brain dead. If we remove the life support machine, we believe that he will die within minutes. We feel that prolonging his life is of no benefit to anybody, least of all Shane. I am sorry."

"Thank you, doctor. I cannot say that I did not expect this news. When do ... do you switch off the machine? Can I have some time with him?"

"Of course," said Dr. Curry. Dan followed Dr. Curry as she walked towards the nurses' station.

"Doctor, with respect to Shane's organ donor card ... I intend to honour his wishes."

"Thank you, Mr. Kinsella."

Dan returned to Shane's bed. Fr. O'Connell retreated. A nurse pulled the curtains around his bed. Dan held Shane's hand.

"I wish I could recite a prayer that describes the great loss I feel. When Deirdre died, we had each other. Now I am to face the future alone. Grief is a natural emotion and I will never fully camouflage the hurt and anger I feel. I can only hope that, in the fullness of time, I will forgive those responsible for taking your life. I love you, son, and I hope that if by chance there is eternal life, we will meet again. I will write to your mother and tell her what a fine young man you were. I will tell her of all the joy and happiness you brought us. I am sorry for her sake that she never met you."

Dan kissed his son, stroked his cheek, then walked swiftly from intensive care. The clock in the reception area pointed to nine a.m.. He paused a moment before he bought a newspaper. Now that the meeting with Dr. Curry was over, Dan regained some measure of reality. In reception, he observed the tide of humanity as it passed by the inane modern stone sculptures lining the way to the service lifts.

Dan nodded to the receptionist as he left the hospital. He went for a walk. He had no idea why or where he was going.

Then he saw the floodlights of Dalymount Park. He was immediately engulfed in memories. The soccer internationals when there were no tickets needed. A Wednesday night. The 46A bus into College Street. The long walk up O'Connell Street. Arriving in Phibsborough at seven-thirty for an eight o'clock kick-off. Standing in the queue, Shane sitting on his shoulders waving his green and white flag and roaring "Ireland! Ireland!". Dan remembered the day the Spanish keeper jumped and caught the ball over the penalty spot. It was from a corner. Before his feet touched the ground, he was shouldered by Charlie Hurley and ended up tangled in the net. He remembered the night Ray Treacy ran around kicking the entire Russian defence, allowing Don Givens to score three goals. The poor Russians were so preoccupied following Treacy around the park that they forgot Givens. Then there was the Cup Final, Shamrock Rovers against Waterford. The splendid hat trick by Mick Leech. The huge crowds in Milltown for the domestic matches. There were thirty-eight thousand people in Dalymount Park for the Cup Final that day and very few actually saw the game it was so crowded.

How things had changed. Dan could no longer get a ticket for the matches. He and Shane watched the matches on the big screen in the Magic Carpet. Now, Dan suddenly realised, that too would no longer be possible.

As he approached the hospital, Dan noticed two men double-parked in a blue Ford Transit van. They were talking to another man in a dark suit. Dan recognised the men in the van as the maintenance men he had met in the intensive care department. They were still dressed in their overalls. Dan nodded at the two men as he passed. They looked away.

"Morning" Dan said to the man in the suit as he eased past him.

The man was Raymond Mackin.

Chapter 19

Dr. Curry turned as her colleague Dr. Brennan burst into her office and informed her that the tests had, astonishingly, matched Shane Kinsella's heart with James Mackin's.

She toyed with the idea of confiding in Dr. Brennan, but declined. She was addled. She had spoken to Fred Hanley, the journalist, the previous night after the intruders had fled. He gave her an insight into how Mackin operated his business. She was somewhat comforted by the fact that she was not the only one who had been snared by Mackin. She was tired and confused, decided not to stay in the apartment and booked into the Killiney Castle Hotel until the locks of the apartment were changed.

Dr. Curry discussed the preparations for the transplant operation with Dr. Brennan. There was an emergency in casualty. Dr. Brennan was paged. He left Dr. Curry pacing her office. Her professional detachment had abandoned her. She was irrevocably torn between both boys. She had fought to save Shane's life on the pavement in Cabinteely while the parish priest had administered the last rites. Now she was about switch off his life support machine, remove his healthy heart and transplant it to James. Could she abandon her professional etiquette and allow Mackin to believe that she had switched off Shane's life support machine to nullify her debt? ... No, she would not jeopardise her career. She had to confront Mackin. She would inform him that even if and when Shane's machine was finally shut down, it was likely that his heart may not be suitable for James. The distribution of donor organs was networked and not within her responsibility.

Dr. Curry entered James Mackin's room. He was

playing cards with one of the nurses.

"Hello, Dr. Curry." James was in cheerful mood.

"Excuse me, nurse. I would like to speak to James."

The nurse left the room and closed the door behind her.

"James, I have some news for you. A donor heart has been made available. We must prepare you for a possible transplant. I should warn you that there are many reasons why the operation may be aborted before you even enter the operating theatre, but we must believe at this juncture that we will go ahead within the next twenty-four hours."

James was speechless. He just lay back on the bed and stared at Dr. Curry.

"I'm not sure, doctor, whether I should be happy."

James began to cry. Dr. Curry moved to the bed to comfort him. They sat in silence. It was a peaceful respite for both. There was a knock on the door. Veronica Mackin entered the room. Dr. Curry stood and detailed the news to her.

"First of all, it will be necessary to move James to an isolation room. Then we can run some further tests to see if he is allergic to any of the anti-rejection drugs. It is all very routine really."

Dr. Curry left the room and continued with her morning rounds. As she neared the neurological wing, she was approached by one of the maintenance men.

"Excuse me, Dr. Curry. I have a message from a friend of mine. He said that your time is running out. He will probably contact you later ... at home."

Dr. Curry returned immediately to the sanctuary of her office. As she opened the door, she saw Raymond Mackin sitting behind her desk. Veronica stood by the window.

"Veronica, I think you had better leave. Dr. Curry and I have some business to discuss."

The unfortunate woman was nothing more than a

puppet in a horrific, real-life drama. Veronica Mackin hated her husband, but was confident that if anyone could find a way to offer life to James he would surely find it. As the door closed, Mackin spoke to Dr. Curry. He was, as ever, controlled but determined.

"You made serious accusations of child abuse against me, doctor. I hope that you have some palpable evidence to back your findings."

Dr. Curry was quite taken aback. For what seemed an eternity, she struggled to find the words to respond. She sat down. Mackin watched her intensely. Dr. Curry's voice shook with uncontrolled anger as she spoke.

"I am James's doctor," she roared, "and, at this moment, I am not prepared to accuse you or anyone else of child abuse. I only ask that you take a good look at yourself and what you have done to possibly the only two people in this world that could love you. James is facing the most critical twenty-four hours of his short life. Whatever about the rest of us, for his sake I had hoped that this subject could have waited until his condition had improved. Be aware that I am bound by law, Mr. Mackin, to report my findings."

"Bound by law?" Mackin queried in a defiant tone.

"Yes, Mr. Mackin. A doctor who discovers clinical evidence of child abuse is obliged to report his findings to the relevant bodies. These matters are dealt with discretely. The intent of the law is not to disgrace the parent, but to protect the child."

"Doctor, I think you are losing sight of your objectives. You are certainly not focused, as you should be, on your personal problems. Until James's transplant becomes a reality, I am of the opinion that you cannot financially afford to make accusations or ignore my proposition. Veronica tells me that there is the possibility of a donor heart being made available. Doctor, excuse me, but I get the distinct impression that my friends and I were not fully understood. There is a donor heart available downstairs in this hospital's intensive care department. It belongs to Shane Kinsella and it's not a possibility. It is a fact. Do I have to ask my colleagues to drop in and visit you again?"

Joan stood and walked over to her desk where Mackin sat. She leaned on the desk and spoke, her voice quivering.

"Mr. Mackin, I will not deny that you frighten me but, believe me, there is something that I fear more."

Dr. Curry turned and walked to the window.

"What I fear most now is losing my self-respect. Recently, I lost the one person that meant more to me than anything else. Now all that I can lose are material possessions — my home and my car. Believe me when I say, Mr. Mackin, I will never compromise my patients. I have studied for many years and have been appointed to watch over the life and health of those in my care. I sincerely hope that the love for my profession will drive me at all times. When I see a patient, my duty is to relieve their pain and not to engage my mind in the pursuit of financial rewards. All I ask for now is the strength, time and opportunity to further my knowledge."

"An impressive oratory, doctor. Your peers would be proud."

Mackin left the office. Dr. Curry continued to pace the room for what seemed an eternity before she dared to venture out to finish her rounds.

CHAPTER 20

Raymond Mackin returned to his office. The receptionist pointed to the man seated in the waiting room.

"I am sorry, Mr. Mackin. He would not allow me to contact you!"

"Who is he?"

The receptionist checked her notepad.

"Detective Inspector Ken Maher of the fraud squad, Harcourt Street."

"Good morning. You were looking for me?" Mackin extended his hand and gestured for the detective to sit down.

"The R.U.C. have sent us a file on a company registered to an Irishman with a postal address in Bolivia. They have asked us to investigate a number of irregularities that appear on contracts issued by this company."

For over an hour, Mackin led the detective around in ever-increasing circles. The man left R.M. & P. content in the knowledge that Mackin was guilty, but incensed that Mackin's greater understanding of the world of finance had rendered the interview useless. In the squad car, the detective radioed an order for round-the-clock surveillance on Raymond Mackin.

In his office, Mackin deliberated. He was confident that he had utterly confused and, at the same time, pacified the fraud squad detective. He was, however, not so certain that the organisation would understand. Mackin picked up his dictaphone.

A letter to Dr. Joan Curry.
The Penthouse,
Killiney Hill Apartments.

Dear Dr. Curry ... no. Dear Joan. That sounds more friendly.

Further to our discussion today. As agreed, in return for your professional services, I have, as suggested, credited your account ...

Mackin picked up Dr. Curry's statement printout and circled a figure with his fountain pen. He stroked his unshaven chin.

... to the sum of twelve thousand pounds.

I would like to thank you most sincerely for offering my son James the opportunity of a new life. You can rest assured that this agreement, due to the extreme sensitivity of its execution, will remain a confidence shared only by your good self and me. While it must be a disturbing and difficult time for Mr. Kinsella, and I am aware that confidentiality between the donor and the transplant patient is paramount, I still wish there was some way of conveying my gratitude to the unfortunate man.

I would like to conclude by stating that I am sincerely sorry that your recent ventures into the stock market have proved unsuccessful. You can rest assured, however, that I will personally monitor your portfolio and, over the coming months, attempt to make good your losses.

Yours sincerely ...

Mackin was delighted with his deception. Within the confines of the letter, he had suggested that Dr. Curry had not only been a willing party, but had also been the instigator of the sale of Shane Kinsella's heart for her own personal gain. Mackin instructed that the letter should be delivered to Dr. Curry's apartment that afternoon. His phone rang. It was the hospital.

"Mr. Mackin, this is Nurse Yeats. I have a call for you." It was Veronica.

"Raymond, James has been moved into the isolation room. I think you should be here."

કે કે કે

At Garda Headquarters, Detective Inspector Ken Maher of the fraud squad made a phone call to Caomhín Ó Dúill.

"Mr. Ó Dúill? This is Detective Inspector Maher of the fraud squad. I am ringing in relation to a conversation I had this morning with a business associate of yours, a Mr. Raymond Mackin of R.M. & P. Stockbrokers. I would like to meet with you. Mr. Mackin has made some serious allegations that I would like you to substantiate."

Maher put down the phone. He was aware that he had set up Raymond Mackin. In doing so, he knew that he would flush out Ó Dúill and effectively reduce the flow of funds and arms to these subversives.

કે કે કે

Mackin left almost immediately for the hospital, followed by an unmarked garda car. His car phone rang. He ignored it. At the hospital Mackin, through force of habit, went directly to James's room. He received a shock when he found the room empty. A nurse came in and led him to the isolation room.

James had already been bathed and scrubbed in an antiseptic solution. Mackin had to put on a surgical gown

108

and mask. Veronica sat next to James. As always, she held his hand. Mackin, for the first time, realised just how beautiful his wife's eyes were. At this moment, they appeared apprehensive but hopeful.

Earlier, James had been tested to see if he was allergic to the anti-rejection drug. Dr. Curry injected a minute drop of the drug into James's left arm. Two small blisters appeared. She drew a ring around them.

"I just want to see if they enlarge," Dr. Curry explained.

Two dots were tattooed, one on James's chest, the other underneath his left armpit.

"This is to indicate where the electrodes are to be attached. I'm sorry, these marks will be with you for life," Dr. Curry said. "From this moment on, you will always be recognised as a heart transplant patient."

A drip was set up containing a drug that would kill off most of James's white blood cells. The drug's function was to suppress the body's natural immunity system and its ability to fight off foreign cells. This drug would prevent the body from rejecting the implanted organ. It was important, however, to leave enough white blood cells to fight off bacteria.

A doctor entered the room and called Mackin to one side.

"Mr. Mackin?" the doctor enquired. "I need to speak to you outside."

Mackin followed the doctor out into the corridor.

"Mr. Mackin, do you know what this is?"

Mackin looked down. It took him a few moments to realise that the man was holding a handgun.

"Mr. Mackin, I earn a lot of money by eliminating people and the problems they create. I am a sort of troubleshooter. The more severe the punishment, the more I earn. The bigger the contract, the larger the commission. As a financial advisor, you will understand what I am talking about. At the moment, my employers are displeased. So am I. It would suit me if you didn't manage to sort out these problems. You have twenty-four hours!"

"What can I do?" Mackin pleaded.

The man ignored his question. He smiled reassuringly and put his arm around Mackin's shoulder. He gestured for him to listen to the advice he was about to give him. Mackin relaxed, turned his head and leaned forward. The man crashed his forehead down on the side of Mackin's temple, sending him sprawling face-down on the grey carpet tiles.

CHAPTER 21

The room was silent. Shane lay motionless on his bed. He was now merely a silhouette of his past. He appeared as an effigy, already resigned to the waxen pallor of death. Dan sat with Fr. O'Connell. They were waiting for Dr. Curry. Dan blocked his memories and rebuked himself for his lack of emotion. The past few days had drained him of all sentiment. He wondered what would become of Shane's organs and would he ever meet the recipient? He looked at his watch. It was just after ten a.m.. He walked to the window and watched as the raindrops ran down the glass in irregular channels. A nurse, head bowed in respect, pulled the curtains around Shane's bed. Dan continued to stare out the window. He wondered how long it had been since the accident. For the past few days, his world had revolved solely around the intensive care ward and the hospital restaurant. He read the newspapers, but digested nothing. It did not matter now. All problems paled into insignificance. In the distance, he could hear a radio programme. The caller was complaining about the cost of local phone calls. Dan looked at Shane. If only that was all he had to worry about. He would pay any price to hear Shane speak again!

Dan's observations were becoming more vivid. It was if he were coming out of the nether world he had retreated into and was now re-establishing himself in the real world. The fog was lifting and the stark reality of what had happened struck him like a bolt of lightning. At first, a single tear appeared in the corner of his eye and trickled down his cheek. Then his emotions exploded in a torrent of pent up anger.

"Shane, I want you to know that you are everything to

me! Without you, my life will have no meaning. I am not a vindictive man, but I vow to search out the men who did this to you. I promise you … an eye for an eye. I will, no matter how long it takes, avenge your death!"

Dan moved to the bed and held Shane's limp head in his arms.

"I want this damn machine turned off. Father, will you fetch Dr. Curry please. I want her to end this masquerade now! I want my son to die with dignity."

Dan's uneasy mind wandered beyond the intensive care department. He caught his breath. He felt a strange presence envelope him. It was as if he too were being cradled in the arms of a calming force. Dan's expression was puzzled. A meaningless smile spread across his thin lips as he stared unseeingly at the ceiling. He could feel the warm sun on his back. July had almost gone. His neck and shoulders were sunburnt. They had been staying in the old caravan in Brittas Bay for almost three weeks now. Deirdre and Dan were in Staunton's field armed with pitch forks. They were turning the hay. Deirdre, her head thrown back, was laughing. The sun reflected upon her long chestnut-coloured hair. Dan put his arm around her thin waist. He felt a great surge of love. They watched Shane. He was fifteen now. He ran from the field to follow the girl riding the pony through the dunes. He had done this every day for the past two weeks. Her father owned the big house on the hill. He was a business man from Dublin. Carol was to become Shane's first love. Dan and Deirdre lay back on the grass, Dan's head resting on her lap. Deirdre stroked his head and ran her fingers through his hair.

"This is a very special moment," she whispered. "Dan, you must believe that Shane and I are part of your soul. Be comforted that we will meet again in another world. This world lies just beyond your understanding. We will be with you always. Good-bye, my love."

"Mr. Kinsella, Dr. Curry phoned down. She will be with you in a few minutes."

Dan shook his head in disbelief. He was stunned. He rubbed his eyes and looked to Fr. O'Connell for an explanation.

"I think we should offer a final prayer for Shane's soul, Dan. Join me."

Dr. Curry entered the cubicle as Fr. O'Connell finished his prayer. Both men stood.

"Mr. Kinsella, there are few words of comfort I can offer. You have, of course, made a difficult and compassionate decision. Please accept my deepest sympathy."

Two nurses entered the cubicle and stood at the end of the bed, their heads bowed in respect. Dan turned to face them. One, a young girl, fought back tears. Fr. O'Connell prayed aloud. Dr. Curry approached the machine and turned the switch. The hiss and click of the machine that had sustained Shane's life fell silent. Dr. Curry swiftly removed all the tubes and sensors, then retreated and stood beside the nurses. Dan noticed that the ward beyond the curtain had gone silent. A crippling pain spread across Dan's spine. Fr. O'Connell put his right arm around his shoulders and pulled him close to him. With his left hand, Dan held onto the priest's coat. Dan held his breath as he watched his son die as he wished, painlessly and with dignity.

After what seemed an eternity, there was an expulsion of air from Shane's ravaged body. Dr. Curry walked to the bed and checked his pulse. She replaced his hand beneath the covers, turned, smiled ruefully and left the cubicle. Fr. O'Connell spoke.

"Shane is no longer of this world, Dan. He gave love freely. Take comfort that he suffers no more."

Dan and Fr. O'Connell left the ward. The young nurse recorded the time of death. A tear fell onto her clipboard and smudged the ink. She wiped it away. Within minutes, an attendant accompanied by another nurse wheeled Shane's rigid body through the labyrinth of back corridors to the service lift. Dr. Brennan and his staff were scrubbed and waiting in the operating theatre.

CHAPTER 22

Dr. Curry and her staff were primed and ready for the operation. The anaesthetist monitored James's heartbeat. It fell. He hooked up a isoprenaline drip to stimulate cardiac contraction and heart rate. James was put on an artificial ventilator. Arterial and venous pressures were monitored by a small cannula in the artery and vein of the wrist and neck respectively. James's temperature was taken from the roof of his mouth. The correct balance of his body chemistry was vital to the success of the operation.

Dr. Curry had explained to Mr. and Mrs. Mackin about the upcoming transplant operation.

"It is a gamble that is not a gamble. Strictly speaking, James's heart can never be restored to its normal function. If he does not undergo a heart transplant within the next three or four weeks, by all probability he could die. What we have here is a duel between life and death with a reward worthy of the challenge. James," she explained, "was unlike most infants born with this particular affliction. He had managed to survive. When he was nothing more than a collection of cells in his mother's womb, something simply went wrong with the cluster that formed his heart."

At ten forty-four a.m., word came through that the donor heart had been successfully removed. Dr. Curry approached the operating table. She called her team together, raised her scalpel and made an incision along the length of James's sternum. She glanced at the large Smith's clock. She had only three hours to perform the operation. Thereafter, the donor heart's energy depleted, rendering it useless.

A junior doctor cut open the breastbone with an oscillating saw. He placed a large retractor into the cavity to force the two halves apart. Eighteen minutes later, the two layers of the pericardium, the membranous sac covering the heart, were carefully opened and all the major vessels prised and cut away from the adjoining tissue.

Dr. Curry was an hour into the operation now. A nurse wiped the sweat from her brow. To prevent blood clotting, Heparin was administered and a large plastic pipe was inserted into the two large veins entering the right side of the heart. A slightly smaller pipe was inserted into the aorta, the main artery from the heart which distributes blood throughout the body. These pipes were then joined to the heart-lung machine.

Dr. Curry still fought with her emotions. In all the time she had studied medicine, nothing had prepared her for what she was about to experience. At exactly mid-day, she removed Shane's heart from the cooling box and trimmed it to size. This was the first time that she had known the donor. This heart was not simply an anonymous organ. It had a personality and an identity. It was a shattering experience.

The heart-lung machine now took over the function from James's organs. From now on, the machine would oxygenate and distribute the blood around his body. Dr. Curry looked at the clock on the wall. A junior doctor, stopwatch in hand, confirmed that the donor heart had been without blood for nearly two hours now. James's body temperature had cooled to almost thirty degrees centigrade.

At a quarter past mid-day, Dr. Curry reached the point of no return. She began to remove the old heart and insert the new. Dr. Curry had left part of the old heart and commenced the laborious job of joining the two hearts.

Thirty minutes later, the stitching was completed. A coolant was circulated around the back of the new heart to prevent it from re-warming. Dr. Curry sighed with relief.

All that remained now was to join up the pulmonary arteries and then those of the aorta, the main artery of the body which transports oxygen-rich blood from the left side of the heart to all parts of the body.

At one o'clock, a small catheter was placed into the apex of the ventricle to effect decompression and to assist in removing air from the lungs. Six minutes later, the clamp was removed from the aorta to allow blood to flow into the arteries. Dr. Curry glanced at the clock again. The heart had now been without a flow of blood for two and a half hours.

The blood was now re-warmed through the heart-lung machine. All the remnants of air were removed from the chambers of the heart using a needle and syringe. At ten past one, the donor heart was in position. All that remained now was to see if Shane's donor heart would respond to stimulation and give life to James.

There was a great air of expectancy in the operating room. All eyes were on Dr. Curry. She stood back and knitted the bloodied fingers of both hands … To the delight of all present, the heart responded immediately to the electric shock. A few small leaks were discovered and were swiftly repaired.

James's donor heart, supported by the heart-lung machine, recovered and the full body-warming process was accomplished. Dr. Curry and her staff now witnessed the miracle of a donor heart coming alive as the blood flow from the heart-lung machine was reduced and James's new heart took over.

At twenty to two, James's heart was pumping at five litres of blood per minute, which was about right for a resting heart. Five minutes later, a pacemaker was inserted, then all the plastic pipes were removed. Dr. Curry inserted chest drains to collect fluid from the chest cavity.

At two fifteen, the chest spreader was removed and the

two halves of the sternum were wired together. First the muscles were stitched, then the skin.

Just after three p.m., James was placed on a gurney which had been swabbed and wheeled back into the isolation room, where he was connected to an artificial ventilator and a vast array of monitoring equipment.

CHAPTER 23

Raymond and Veronica Mackin sat in James's room. Veronica tried not to look beyond the present. She reflected. Her mind stumbled over her life. She removed the dried red rose from her handbag and held it to her cheek. She examined and speculated how another woman might respond to a man like Raymond Mackin. She looked at her husband watching television. He does not love me, she thought. ... He never loved me. Once, he coveted me. I was young, beautiful and desirable. Once, I could help and console him when he was down, laugh with him when he was happy.

There was no hope. On reflection, she should have walked away from him years ago when he had made her place their son for adoption. Love was blind. For years they have lived a lie.

Dr. Curry entered the room. Veronica looked at her watch. It was eight p.m.. Dr. Curry looked tired and drawn, but she smiled.

"The operation was a success. James is stable. You may visit him now for a few minutes. Remember, he has undergone a very exhausting operation. He may not appear lucid and may float in and out of consciousness. We must hope that the anti-rejection drugs do their job. If they do, then I am confident that James can look forward to a normal life."

≈ ≈ ≈

James Mackin slipped in and out of consciousness. Thankfully, he recognised the faces floating around the end of his bed. He felt no pain. For the first time in as long as he could remember, his breathing was clear. He tried to cough up sputum. To his delight, he couldn't. All the noises in the room were exaggerated. It seemed as if everyone was shouting. He watched as his mother and father put on surgical gowns, masks and gloves before they were allowed to see him. He looked at his fingers and skin. They were now pink and healthy. Before, they were blue and lifeless.

ea ea ea

Dan Kinsella took a taxi home. The full consequences of Shane's death became apparent as the battered old taxi rattled its way through Donnybrook, Mount Merrion and Stillorgan on the journey to Cornelscourt. In Donnybrook, Dan remembered the cold damp winter afternoons he had spent watching Shane, caked in mud, playing rugby in the Leinster schools rugby cups. In Mount Merrion, he recalled the night there was a row outside the old Stella Cinema and how Shane had been wrongfully arrested for disturbing the peace. He could still see Shane's forlorn, nervous face in the interview room in Blackrock Garda Station. As he passed Stillorgan, he could almost smell the wonderful chips they used to devour outside Libro's.

At home in his modest council house in Cornelscourt, Dan Kinsella stood in his son's bedroom looking into his wardrobe. He selected the suit that he wanted Shane to be buried in. They had bought it for his interview with the College of Surgeons. Dan held the suit to his cheek and carried it downstairs. He picked up the post from the mat behind the door and went back outside. The taxi driver was waiting, his engine running. They headed back into the hospital. Dan opened a letter addressed to Shane.

ea ea ea

James did not recognise the young African doctor addressing him.

"Don't worry, James. It is a simple test. If you feel any pain, just squeeze the nurse's hand."

Nurse Yeats smiled and pulled up a chair. She sat down beside James and held his hand. The doctor took a piece of plastic tubing and placed it in James's jugular vein. Then he eased a bioptone through to his heart. He took snips of the heart and muscles to check if there were any signs of rejection. The doctor even wheeled the television screen around so James could see what he was doing.

"I must be careful, James. If I take a wrong turning, I could touch a vein wall and you will probably get a jolt. Do you have any discomfort?"

"Just a slight ache, doctor ... that's all. Just a slight ache."

&. &. &.

Through force of habit, Joan Curry parked her car in front of the apartment block. She hadn't had time to have the locks changed on the doors so she collected the post and booked into the Killiney Castle again. After dinner, she ordered a glass of brandy and read her post. The electricity, gas and phone bills were ignored, as was a letter from the bank. What caught her attention was a hand-delivered envelope. She opened it. Inside was Mackin's letter. She read it in disbelief. To her annoyance, Mackin had worded the letter to sound like she had conspired with him to trade Shane's heart to clear her debt with R.M. & P.. She was incensed and ran from the dining room. At reception, she rang Mackin's office. It was too late. It was closed. She found his home number in the phone book. The answering machine was on. She rang the hospital. Nurse Yeats confirmed that Mackin was with his wife in James's room.

Without further consideration, Joan ran from the hotel. She crossed to the car park, unlocked her Mazda and drove at speed towards the hospital. She found Veronica Mackin alone in James's room. She still clutched the red rose. Mackin had just left. Dr. Curry sat down opposite Veronica. She too was weary.

"You should get some rest!" Dr. Curry advised.

"I could say the same to you, doctor," Veronica Mackin responded. "You look exhausted. I was told you had gone home hours ago."

"I had," Dr. Curry answered. "Something unexpected turned up."

Veronica handed Dr. Curry a letter.

"It is a letter from my son," she explained, "the one that was put up for adoption."

Dr. Curry read the letter.

I have begun writing this letter not knowing what I want to say. Or how I should say it. Maybe it is a cry from a tortured heart searching for solace. I don't really know.

My adopted mother died earlier this year. She had cancer of the throat. It was a great shock. I still miss her. There has been a void in my life since I was old enough to understand that I was adopted. I always wondered under what circumstances I was offered up for adoption. I like to believe that I was loved and that the need for my adoption was forced upon you. I have a re-occurring nightmare of a young woman, her face veiled, crying as she walks down a long, tiled corridor. I see a nun offering the woman a fountain pen and a sheet of parchment paper. The woman is shaking her head.

I can understand that, after eighteen years, my re-birth

could be part of something that you wish to forget. I
sincerely hope not. I enclose my address and a current
photograph. If you have the time, I would love to hear from
you.

The photograph fell into Dr. Curry's lap. She picked it
up and looked at the the smiling boy. She looked back at
the signature on the letter.

Your son,
Shane Kinsella

CHAPTER 24

As Raymond Mackin was about to leave the hospital, his mobile phone rang. It was Dermot Glanville from the stock exchange.

"Raymond, I have been trying to get you all day. A detective from the fraud squad interviewed me in the exchange this afternoon. He asked me to comment on a number of other contracts issued by R.M. & P.. Raymond, I think …"

Mackin snapped the phone shut and turned off the power. Looking through the glass sliding doors in the hospital reception, he noticed a Ford Transit van parked outside the hospital. He recognised the driver. Immediately, he turned and walked back through the reception, out through a fire exit and into the lane at the back of the hospital. He stood back to allow an ambulance to drive out, then walked around to Dorset Street. He stood a moment in the shadows of Bermingham's public house, then slipped into the lounge bar. He ordered a gin and tonic and a toasted cheese sandwich. There was a football match on the television.

Mackin sat facing the door. As he raised the glass to his lips he noticed that his hands were shaking. He downed the drink in one gulp and ordered another.

"Make it a large one!" he added.

With the aid of a bottle of gin, Mackin faced the stark reality that over the past week his personal and business life had careered out of control. He accepted that he had made an error of judgement with Noreen Harte and Bernard Hannigan. He was confident, though, that the newspaper would not print the story. It couldn't afford the loss of revenue from R.M. & P.'s advertising budget. They can report the news, but not create it. The editor was firstly responsible to his board of directors. The fact that he was also a journalist was secondary. The stock exchange would hold an enquiry. Privately, the president of the exchange will suggest that he should go to ground and refrain from high profile activities. Publicly, they would announce that they had found no irregularities. The truth was that the exchange embraced and protected its members and, when necessary, covered them in protective blankets. Mackin's practices were common in stockbroking. It was only his management style that was uncommon. He laughed when he thought of Dr. Curry's inane and naive letter to the stock exchange. She thought that she was the only one who had ever complained. Mackin decided that he would compose a letter for Glanville to send to her.

It would appear, Dr. Curry, that you accepted the deal at the time and, accordingly, we consider that R.M. & P. cannot be held liable for any subsequent fall in value of the shares.

He remembered his cousin John's wife's threat:
"Mr. Mackin, the fruit in your orchard is diseased. My advise to you is don't park your car in a back street. Don't even get out of it at night to close your gates. Not tonight! Not ever!"
His wife Veronica was something he could not control. This was an emotional, not a physical, problem. She was slow and calculated and could prove difficult. He did not love her, but he respected and feared her ability to walk away with half of what he owned. Mackin would not admit, even to himself, that he was worried about the men in the van. He believed somehow that they would just go away.
He abandoned his stool and went to the toilet. He was a

little unsteady on his feet. On his way back, he picked up the public phone and rang Dr. Curry's home number. The answer machine clicked in.

"I'm sorry, I cannot come to the phone at the moment. If you would like to leave your name and number, I will get back to you as soon as possible. Thank you."

"Raymond Mackin here, doctor. I just called to say hello. I presume you got my letter. I have just left James. He seems well. You must have done a reasonable job. I wonder will he live as long as me?"

Mackin laughed. He could never be sure that Dr. Curry had, in fact, transplanted Dan Kinsella's son's heart. He did not care. All that mattered was that the doctor had provided a healthy donor heart.

"I am glad that you decided to take the money. Don't worry about the medical ethics. If you can live with the knowledge, that is all that counts. You needed the money. So welcome to the real world. You had better hope that Dan Kinsella doesn't find out, though. He won't be too happy that you sold his son's heart. I had better go now. Good night and sweet dreams."

CHAPTER 25

D an switched on the light in the taxi and read the letter addressed to Shane. It was from a woman called Veronica Armitage. She must have done well for herself, he thought. The address was Killross House, Stepaside.

Dear Shane,

Despite what you think, I was delighted to receive your letter. I, too, wondered whatever became of you. I was afraid to go looking in case you rejected me. You must believe that it was not my decision to have you adopted. I kept you for over three months after you were born. I was not married at the time and my future husband, Raymond, insisted that you should be put up for adoption. You must understand that in those days it was not acceptable to have an unmarried mother in the family.

The nightmare you speak of in your letter is a frightening reality. It details the night in Cork that I handed you up to the Mother Superior for adoption.

Shane, I apologise. I am writing this letter in hospital. James, my son, is being prepared for an important operation. He has suffered from a congenital heart problem since birth and tomorrow we hope he will undergo a heart transplant operation. The doctor is confident. It just seems sad that one young man must die to give life to another! Please say a prayer for your brother!

Your mother,
Veronica Armitage

Dan fought back the tears. If the poor woman only knew that Shane, the son she had lost and just found, was now dead in the hospital morgue.

The taxi stopped in front of the hospital. Fr. O'Connell was right. Contacting Veronica Armitage while Shane lay on his deathbed would have subjected the unfortunate woman to unnecessary trauma, especially when her other son was undergoing heart surgery.

In the hospital shop, Dan bought a large box of chocolates, then went up to the nurses' station for the last time. He left Shane's suit with one of the nurses. He felt awkward and self-conscious. Before, he had plenty to talk about. Now, he just wanted to get away from the hospital. After thanking the nurses, he almost ran from the hospital. He did not want to go home, so he walked around the corner into Dorset Street . He entered the first pub he came to. Outside, sitting in a Ford Transit van, were the two men he had seen Raymond Mackin talking to the previous day.

❧ ❧ ❧

The lounge door opened. Raymond Mackin glanced over nervously. He thought he recognised the man at the door. He was not sure. The man looked in his direction. Mackin stood and beckoned him to join him.

"Will you have a pint?" Mackin could not think of the man's name.

"Thanks very much, Mr. Mackin. I will have a Guinness."

Dan could see that Mackin was quite drunk.

"Are you celebrating, Mr. Mackin?"

"Is it that obvious? As a matter of fact, I am. My son James underwent a successful heart transplant operation this afternoon. My wife Veronica is with him at the moment."

Dan could not believe what he was hearing. He sat bolt upright. Surely, it was not possible. He excused himself and went to the toilet. He read the letter again. The woman's name was Veronica, but not Mackin. Armitage. The boy's name, however, was James and the father's name was Raymond.

Mackin finished his gin and tonic and ordered another. He was quite drunk now and began to ramble. Dan returned and climbed back up on his stool.

"You know what? This city is my orchard and I have reached out and gathered the fruit from its branches. The same fruit is there for everyone, that is if they are not afraid to climb the ladder."

Mackin took another sip from his glass.

"I am afraid of no man ... or woman for that matter. There is this woman doctor..."

Mackin, his head almost resting on the rim of his glass, pointed towards the hospital at the back of the pub.

"Curry is her name. She needed a little persuasion. My son James is her patient, you see. She told us that he needed an urgent heart transplant. If he didn't, he would be dead within three or four weeks. It is a simple enough operation, she explained. That is, if you can find a suitable donor heart. I told the doctor where she could find one. She explained to me that what I was suggesting was morally wrong, so I sent a few friends of mine to remind her that she owed me twenty grand and she had no choice in the matter.Money can buy you anything in this city. All she had to do was switch off the machine of a young man injured in a car accident near Cornelscourt and transplant his heart to James. He was brain dead and didn't need his heart anyway."

Dan could not believe what he was hearing. Mackin continued to stare into his drink.

"Today she saw reason and switched off the machine and ..."

"A question, Mr. Mackin. What is your wife's maiden name?"

"Armitage. Why?"

Mackin turned to look at Dan. A cold realisation washed over him as he now recognised the man sitting beside him.

Dan considered if what Mackin was saying was true, that Dr. Curry had accepted money to switch off Shane's life support machine and give life to Mackin's son James. If Veronica Armitage is James's mother, then Shane and James were actually brothers and Mackin had ordered the death of his first-born son, Shane.

Dan recalled the deathbed vow he made to Shane:

"I will, no matter how long it takes, avenge your death!".

He got down of his stool and kicked it across the bar. He lunged at Mackin as he nervously raised his glass to his lips. Mackin fell heavily to the floor. The glass shattered. They rolled around on the tiled floor, slamming their fists into each other. Dan's straining fingers found Mackin's throat. He grasped a sliver of broken glass. In fear, Mackin wrestled desperately. He raised his knee and shot it upwards. Dan relaxed his grip. Mackin rolled sideways and pulled himself erect. They watched each other for a moment, saying nothing. They were both breathing hard. Two bar staff vaulted over the counter with baseball bats. Dan and Mackin were easily and forcibly ejected into Dorset Street. The two men, who had been waiting patiently in the van outside Bermingham's, zipped up their anoraks.

❧ ❧ ❧

130

Dr. Curry slept in her office that night. She had hoped that Raymond Mackin would return. She was wrong. At seven a.m., she drove home. In Blackrock, she bought a newspaper. Her mind was still wrestling with the fact that, unwittingly, she had transplanted Shane's heart to his brother James. She could never explain to Veronica Mackin that the heart of the son she had put up for adoption eighteen years ago now gave life to his younger brother.

In the apartment, she made a pot of tea and toast. She put her feet up and opened the paper. The headline read in bold letters;

Dublin Stockbroker found dead in Phoenix Park

Early this morning, Raymond Mackin, a young Dublin stockbroker was found murdered in the Phoenix Park close to Ashtown gate. Mr. Mackin's partially clothed body was found hidden in the bushes by a park attendant. A reliable witness suggested that the crazed murderer had tried to hack Mr. Mackin's heart out with a blunt instrument. The Gardai suspect that the killing is linked to ...

Joan stared at the headline in disbelief. She read the story again, put the paper down and went into her bathroom for a shower. As she passed the telephone, she noticed that the answering machine was flashing. There was a message. Joan reached to press the play button.

᪥ ᪥ ᪥

The detective ordered the uniformed gardai to break down the door. As it splintered open, the distinct odour of death filled their lungs.

"Must be dead over a week now," the detective

guessed, placing a handkerchief over his mouth and picking up an empty pill box lying close to the rapidly decomposing body.

"Nice place isn't it?" a young, uniformed garda commented, fighting back nausea. "Look, sir, there is a message on the answering machine."

The detective pressed the play button.

Raymond Mackin here, doctor. I just called to say hello. I presume you got my letter. I have just left James. He seems well. You must have done a reasonable job. I wonder will he live as long as me? I'm glad that you decided to take the money. Don't worry about the medical ethics. If you can live with the knowledge, that is all that counts. You needed the money. So welcome to the real world. You had better hope that Dan Kinsella doesn't find out, though. He won't be too happy that you sold his son's heart. I had better go now. Good night and sweet dreams.